By Sebastian Black

CharmD Saga
Oathsworn

Published by Dreamspinner Press
www.dreamspinnerpress.com

Oathsworn

Sebastian Black

DREAMSPINNER PRESS

Published by
DREAMSPINNER PRESS

5032 Capital Circle SW, Suite 2, PMB# 279, Tallahassee, FL 32305-7886 USA
www.dreamspinnerpress.com

Trade Paperback ISBN: 978-1-64108-673-8
Digital ISBN: 978-1-64108-672-1
First Edition published by Dreamspun Beyond, December 2020
Trade Paperback published August 2023
Second Edition
v. 2.0

Printed in the United States of America
∞

I'm dedicating this book to all of the unpublished novelists. All you need to succeed is hard work, persistence, and patience.

ACKNOWLEDGMENTS

SUE BROWN-MOORE—THE ridiculously creative and eagle-eyed editor who has a passion for nurturing new writers. Without her tireless help, I wouldn't have gotten far. Thank you for believing in me before I believed it could really happen.

Kat Silver—the brilliantly sharp and extremely talented upcoming author of Dark Flame. This book wouldn't be half as interesting if it weren't for her voice of inspiration. Thanks for grounding me when I needed it most.

Zac—the most tolerant and supportive partner I could ask for. This book wouldn't be possible if it weren't for him. I appreciate your continual patience as much as your uncanny ability to retain my sanity and keep meltdowns at bay.

CHAPTER ONE

FINN TRIED not to look at the mirror as he climbed out of the shower one cautious limb at a time. An unseen force tugged at him—something akin to curiosity, but way stronger. Desperation, perhaps. It was impossible not to steal a glance.

"Dammit." His gaze flitted toward the misted silver, and his heart fell out of his ass onto the cold marble floor. There was another note etched in steam.

This was the fourth day running since a series of messages had stared materializing from nowhere. The newest note read, *Hello…? #Rude.*

Hashtags? Seriously? Clearly it was the work of an imbecile.

Finn Anderson had lived alone for the last seven years, and that suited him just fine. He'd loathed sharing his personal space ever since the cramped college dorm in Tulsa. He valued his privacy so much he never bothered to employ a maid, much to his family's annoyance. Money wasn't the issue—he could hire the entire staff of the Four Seasons for a solid year, no sweat. Finn just didn't want anyone in *his* space.

Nobody except his Realtor had even seen this new place, and he doubted the elderly British lady was to blame for this invasion of privacy. Besides, he'd already changed the locks.

So far the notes on his mirror had been harmless on the face of it, ranging from *Hi* to *How are you?* and even *I don't wish to upset you.* But somebody was violating his privacy by playing some kind of stupid childish joke, and that was dangerous. Social media talked about stalkers doing this kind of thing all the time, that this type of behavior was almost always a precursor to something more extreme.

Finn let the thought trail off before it spiraled somewhere sinister. Too many *Saw* movies and scaremongering news presenters were starting to get to him.

This was just a prank—by one of his friends no doubt. When he worked out who it was, he'd repay them in kind.

The memory of the first note was forever branded into his brain. He'd gone to fetch a towel from the warmer, only to gape at the word *Hello?* smudged finger-paint style in the vapor. Gooseflesh had worked its way up his spine, but he merely laughed it off and called out, "Ha-ha very funny!"

Finn waited for an answer, although a sensible reaction would've been to sprint through his place and call the police. But at the time, it felt like overkill.

In hindsight maybe he should have.

Living in an upper-class New York penthouse meant he could avoid the streets below, and any conflict in his life was limited to the workplace. He rationalized the first message as a figment of his imagination—just work stress driving him loopy. But now that a fifth note had appeared during his postwork shower, Finn weighed his options.

He could give in to fear and summon the cops, but they'd only reassure him there had been no forced entry or other sign of a break-in. The alarm would have gone off, right? Twice he'd conducted a search of his apartment, stark naked, and it proved the same thing both times. He'd been alone then, and he was alone now.

Instead of acting like a CSI intern, he wiped the message off with a face towel and refused to admit it bothered him. Out of sight, out of mind.

Fixing himself three fingers of a smooth eighteen-year-old bourbon, Finn gazed at the twinkling lights that sprawled beyond the enormous window. Powerlessness was not a familiar feeling, and it bothered him how something so minor could have such an effect on his psyche.

It wasn't normal for him to drink to excess—especially on a weekday—but Finn managed to put the ideas of ghosts and poltergeists to bed after his fourth tumbler. Wobbly and somewhat content, the incident was all but forgotten until the next day, when he threw on some sweatpants and glanced at the mirror en route to the kitchen.

Though the mirror was clear of steam and messages, thoughts of supernatural entities or strangers running rampant through his apartment came back with a vengeance. He couldn't shake the unnerving feeling, even as he cracked eggs into a glass and sprinkled on some protein powder. After whipping it up with a fork, he downed it.

Wincing, he chased it with some water. Raw eggs are something his palate could never quite get used to no matter how much good they did for his body.

Getting a purpose in mind, he paced over to the window and clapped twice to get some jazz going overhead. When he climbed onto the elliptical and pushed Go, his presets sprang to life, and in the rising sun, he felt his abs pinch from yesterday's workout.

Finn worked up a light sweat within a few minutes, but he dialed it up a few gears and felt the notches click as he adjusted the machine for the hell of it. A hardcore workout as the city woke up was better than psychoanalyzing past events. It wasn't long before Finn found himself in a good headspace to carry on with his day. It was time to think about work.

As soon as he graduated college, his parents had funded his startup for a food magazine primarily focusing content on locally grown produce. Things went smoothly enough in the paper editions… but when *Zest* had to join the rest of the digital world and include the function to curate a home-delivered organic food box, Finn had to hire a handful of employees to help manage the code for the carefully constructed framework.

That had been okay for a time too, especially when clickable celebrity cameos provided healthy ad revenue, but the increased demand for mobile apps weighed heavy on Finn. Paper editions of cuisine journalism were quickly becoming relics of the past, and it didn't sit well that nobody cared to pay attention to anything unless it was squished onto smartphone screens.

The app never held much charm for Finn, and his father's motto of "It's just good business" played on a loop as he ramped up the resistance dial.

The company eventually expanded, but Finn's productivity began to wane when they hired Gabriel Fernandez. The annoyingly attractive expat was set on acquiring high-profile chefs to brag about the farm-to-table app, but Finn wanted local heroes to shine. A TV *personality* was just that, on the face of it, and he found them to be absolute divas to work with.

He needed some new talent, like yesterday, and he was working more days and longer hours than ever before now that his parents were threatening to pull the plug on his brainchild. If he didn't come up with something immediately, his career was in the can. He'd be damned if anything got in his way. Whether the magazine was ported to an app or not, he had to make his idea a success and prove them all wrong.

Failing and humiliating his parents wasn't an option, not after they'd worked three jobs each to put him through college, not after Finn literally begged them to fund his startup after their potluck investment with Bitcoin—the cash from which they used to get into real estate that paid dividends in the form of a handsome fortune. Since then, money was all they cared about, and Finn had worked all his adult life to run his own business. There had to be a way to gain back the edge.

Blinking back sweat, he eyed the clock in the corner of the elliptical and realized it was well past time to leave. Finn's body clock was usually a sure thing when he was able to focus solely on work, but while he punished his body, his thoughts drifted to the mysterious messages, and getting sidetracked screwed up his mental schedule.

Scrambling about his place, Finn was the literal embodiment of a hot mess, but the mere thought of showering set him on edge. Yet it had to be done. It took all he had to avoid the mirror, but he threw a towel over it and jumped in for a good scrub. As he lathered up, Finn noticed through the frosted glass that the towel was lying crumpled on the floor. Heart pounding, he was so on edge he could only stand to wash the important bits.

"Um," he breathed, "fuck that shit."

He dashed out of the cubicle, grabbed a new towel off the rack, made a break for the bedroom, and dried himself there. Then he selected a freshly pressed suit, but a headache loomed even before he drenched himself in his favorite cologne.

There was a fresh pack of Tylenol in his wallet, so he popped some. Then he jogged downstairs because his personal elevator was still out of service. He'd have to chase them down again on that, but his main priority was ordering an Uber. Tardiness was among a long list of slipups lately, and Finn wasn't much looking forward to what the day had in store for him.

IT WAS his habit to leave early enough to hop on the subway, but today Finn threw himself into the back of a dusty Prius and held a stop-hand to the driver. His destination was already prearranged by another marvel of modern technology, and he had zero interest in small talk.

With clammy fingers, he whipped out his phone and dialed his Realtor.

"I'm afraid we're unable to relocate you to a new property, Mr. Anderson," crooned a soft yet poignant Irene Blakely. The clean accent was usually a comfort, but this was bad news. Finn had charmed her into letting him hop apartments when he disliked the bigoted neighbors in his last place. He'd pictured himself and the Realtor becoming fast friends, but any hope of that was tossed out the grime-slicked window.

"And why is that?" he asked, unable to keep the desperation out of his voice. "Something has come up. I hate it there. I'll wire you $10k if you can move me before tonight."

"You entered a legal agreement, and I warned you rushing the latest move might have consequences. This clause was one of them." She put on her most caring voice, but Finn imagined a smug smile behind the corded desk phone. "I would have thought you, of all people, would know the severity of binding contracts."

"Yes, well, I—you—" He grasped at air for something to say. He hadn't stammered like that since he was nine years old and struggling to recite a poem at the county fair. "I'm not impressed."

"I understand. And yet some things are simply beyond our control." Again, he detected hints of a smile. She hadn't missed a beat despite his undertone. "You relocated less than a week ago. Perhaps you could just try and settle in?"

Irene was used to dealing with rich people every day. He couldn't exactly tell her the need to move was down to a wanton ghost.

"Okay, thirty thousand?" he ventured. Nobody in their right mind could turn that down.

After a pause she continued, "It appears you secured our last penthouse. Nothing is available that meets your specifications, not for the next four months, at least."

Defeated, Finn sighed. The last thing he wanted was to abandon his principles and rent a crappy second condo somewhere else. He'd lived in multiple houses as a kid, but as an adult, he had to be grounded in one place.

"There's got to be some wiggle room," he pressed. His parents had always taught him there weren't many problems cash couldn't solve. That or the promise of a tarnished reputation. "Is there nothing you can do?"

"Afraid not." Her tone was final. "We don't deal in cash, regardless of circumstance. My hands are tied. I'm sorry."

Finn silenced her with a decisive button press, pissed off enough to bark at the driver. Stepping on the gas was obviously useless; they were caught in the midmorning commuter jam and were getting nowhere fast.

Paranoia poked at him with ice-cold fingers. He couldn't help wondering if Irene knew about the messages. Was she in cahoots with someone? Maybe it was Gabriel throwing him off so he could finally swoop in and take over the business and make Finn look incompetent in the same breath. The guy was childish enough, sure, but did he have the resources to track down Irene and get her involved?

If he didn't get a handle on the situation, he'd either lose his job or find himself carted off in a straitjacket.

When the driver finally found the drop-off point, Finn became hyperaware of his appearance. The paisley tie was skewed where he'd rushed, and because he hadn't managed a deep scrub like normal, the heat of the cab had built up sweat. Being the founder, he was intolerant of shabbiness, and he himself had set the bar for the office dress culture. He'd let people go in the past solely due to inappropriate clothing, so he knew better than anyone the unspoken rule of attire and hygiene. Since his desk was on the top floor, right at the back of an open-plan team of twenty astute individuals, plus all the door staff and the elevator steward—not to mention the interns—he'd have to walk past at least forty people smelling like a foot.

"Good morning, Mr. Anderson," Shelly greeted him as he walked onto the floor. She was a promising PA in her midtwenties who never went a day without her blond hair tied up in a classy chignon. When Finn nodded his head, she misjudged the reserved greeting as permission to walk alongside him.

"I've collated the transcriptions for The Spotted Pig sous-chef interview." She shuffled a stack of papers and matched his brisk pace. "He shed a lot of light on their work ethics. It'll make for an interesting read."

"Good." Finn was curt, eyes fixed on his office. As well as not properly washing, he hadn't managed to brush his teeth, so he was careful to angle his breath away from her. There were at least three sticks of gum in his desk drawer and a fresh deodorant can. They were top priority.

"Also, Gabe wants to talk to you, Mr. Anderson. Should I send him through?"

Shit. Another question that demanded a verbal response. He threw a low-armed salute to the rest of his team as he passed them, but Shelley stopped outside his office while his hand rested on the doorknob. He would sooner nod than speak, but they were in a professional work environment, not kindergarten.

"Yes. But you and I both know Mr. Fernandez hates it when people call him that."

"Yep." She grinned mischievously before a frown marred her oval face. They stood close, and he started to doubt the effectiveness of the cologne he'd bathed in.

Shelly's expression was replaced by an automatic smile, and when she spun on her heels to sashay away, Finn dove into his office and fumbled with the lock on his desk drawers. He ransacked them, drenched his suit in half the bottle of spray, and chomped on a stick of gum like it was a fillet steak.

Pointless, perhaps, but image was essential, now more than ever.

No more than two minutes had passed before Gabriel burst through his door. Finn had just sat behind his desk to survey a mountain of time-sensitive tasks on his PC, and he suppressed a roaring laugh when his rival started a sneezing fit. He hoped it was loud enough to upset the office floor and deduct a few imaginary points.

"Geez," Gabriel managed through his clearly now-exaggerated coughs. "Did the pretty boy fart or something? Could've just lit a candle instead of trying to gas the place."

"Hilarious," Finn deadpanned.

Gabriel was hot in an obvious know-it-all sort of way, what with the square jaw and thick, glossy platinum hair he'd inherited from his Scandinavian ancestors. But any thoughts Finn had of crushing on a frenemy were long past. He hadn't fantasized about what he'd do to the body underneath the three-piece since he realized the man was sent by his parents to *salvage* his company. As though he'd been doing that bad a job. It was fucking typical of them to be so dramatic.

Irrespective of the gulf between them, Gabriel was also too domineering. Finn liked his guys a little softer around the edges.

"Have you seen Madison's latest email?"

"Not yet." Clicking through the intranet, he slid his hands over the keyboard to access the admin server of *Zest*. "I'm uploading the financial projections."

"Well ticktock, Finny boy." Ever the showman, Gabriel pulled back the cuff of his suit and tapped a finger on his white-gold Cartier watch. After grinding his way from a hard-up background, he was never shy about letting everyone know just how far he'd come. "You realize the rest of the board is bound to have noticed how many times you've been late this week? I sure have."

Heaving a pointed sigh, he finally met the man's arrogant stare. *The board* was code for Finn's parents, who helped run the firm from the comfort of their mansion in Tulsa, and he didn't appreciate the reminder that both Gabriel and he were vying for creative control.

"I've been here an hour already," Gabriel continued with feigned nonchalance, taking time to stroll about the office and survey the classic Warhol pieces. The Campbell Soup and green Coca-Cola replicas were among Finn's favorites, but he doubted his rival could appreciate their minimalist beauty. "Just uploaded seven draft posts and put in two more high-profile interviews for request. Even made coffee rounds for the whole team."

That *was* impressive, but he would rather eat his unwashed hair than say so.

"I like to believe my talents lie elsewhere, Gabe." Gabriel snorted at the abbreviation—exactly the anticipated reaction. "Before you muscled on in here, my job was to lead the engineering team and create new code. Now I'm stuck here thinking up bullshit ways to entice all the screen-scrolling zombies out there. I swear it's like no one has their own brain anymore. More to the point, don't interns make coffee?"

"Community is all the rage these days," said Gabriel. "It'll give me the edge when the time comes."

"Sure," Finn snarked. The cell in his pocket vibrated, and he was surprised to find his mom's name flashing on the screen.

He ignored it. They weren't scheduled to talk for another three weeks. Not outside of prearranged business meetings, anyway.

Gabriel was still gazing at him, smugness toxifying the air like bug repellent. But Finn had reached his limit. "Do you have anything important to say, or did you just barge in here to throw me off?"

Shrugging, his rival made his intentions known. "We've been summoned to another board meeting."

Rolling his eyes, he huffed a sigh at his computer screen.

"I know," Gabriel agreed. "Third one this month. But I hear Finn Senior will be attending via satellite. Should be a hoot."

At the mere mention of his father, a cold hand slapped Finn across the face. Instinctively he sat up straighter, already feeling his spirit waning. The thought of spending another half hour alongside Gabriel was enough to make him woozy… let alone being subject to another of his father's famous lectures.

"Ticktock," Gabriel said again, brandishing his watch one more time. "Meeting is in, oh, sixteen minutes. Oops."

"But I've still got to upload a mountain of projections!"

Hand on the door, Gabriel offered a parting wink. "Then you'd better stop eyeing me up and get to work."

TAPPING THE tip of his pen on his notebook, Finn watched the moisture from a jug of water run down the glass and pool on the aluminum tray.

For the first time in what felt like forever, he was grateful the meeting room was a purposefully cold place. The virtually clinical office was the sole purpose of the entire floor, and though the AC was cranked to the max to encourage alertness, the frigid air wasn't keeping Finn's natural odor at bay as Gabriel and Madison flirted in not-so-hushed tones.

"I loved that article you wrote the other day," she said. From the corner of his eye, she tossed brunet waves over her shoulder and leaned in closer. "Especially the part about *firm* eggplants."

At this point, their innuendos were blatant and beyond careless. There had been undeniable lust ricocheting between them for months, and there was no doubt the pair were making googly eyes at each other as they waited for the CEO to grace them with his presence.

Finn was never sure which of his rival's priorities was center stage—taking the limelight from him or screwing the assistant he'd gone out of his way to hire.

Suddenly a bright light preceded an unpleasant chime, and the room was lit with a sky-blue veil as Avery Anderson's face appeared on a screen before them.

Finn's dad had always been a purveyor of all things modern, and the pricey video-calling service was his favorite method of communication. Nobody had the balls to tell him about the latency issues. Even in grainy digital form, the no-nonsense set of his brow and piercing green eyes instantly commanded the room, and everybody corrected their posture instinctively.

"Great to see y'all hard at work," he flatlined. Finn heard Madison's slight intake of breath and didn't bother to turn to see her cheeks go rosy. A bookmaker would go nuts for her predictability. "You got those interviews set up for me, Gabriel?"

"Yes, sir," Gabriel answered without a beat. The stark difference in his persona when the big bad boss was around never ceased to amaze, and it gave Finn some ammunition for later. "I am having difficulty getting Tony Hemsley on board. Says he doesn't want us poking our nose in his business."

"Not good." Avery shook his head and clicked his tongue. There was a slight delay in the feed, so it ended up sounding like a cicada instead of the impatience of a man always on the go. "We need to keep securing these big shots if we want any real interest. The domino effect will be astronomical. And what about you, boy?"

Finn's heart sunk at the nickname. He'd rebuked his father numerous times before—even went as far as to say he wouldn't attend meetings if his dad continued to condescend to him. And yet he'd probably be homeless were it not for his parents. This was a last-ditch attempt to make something of the idea they were funding.

"I just uploaded the financial projections." He closed his eyes and pinched the bridge of his nose, hesitant to follow through. He knew the implications. "If we don't get some investors interested in the magazine this month, we'll have to take out another loan."

"Right, then." Avery took a lengthy pause, and Gabriel's linen pants scratched against his skin where he bounced them up and down. "Y'all know the score, and you've got some decisions to make. Either prove to me that local talent is enough to start earning big bucks, or Gabriel has the green light to start bringing in some big names. Then we use them to push more ads."

Gabriel and Madison exhaled simultaneously, faces undoubtedly smug. It wouldn't be long before they could put their generic, unexciting masterplan into action.

"But wha–"

"No *buts*, Finn." Avery's distorted voice was stern, unwillingly casting him back to times he wasn't allowed to stay out past ten—even at house parties. "Remember that this is a business—cash comes first, thought-provoking content second."

Finn shook his head slowly. He was pissed. What his father was saying made sense… but that didn't mean he had to like it. Blood boiled underneath his skin as he rose to his feet.

"If you want higher revenue, maybe you could come visit in person instead of wasting money on premium communication facilities?"

Whether Finn actually wanted a personal visit or not didn't matter. He knew the device was a distancing tactic to remind everyone who was really in charge, but Finn was tired of footing the blame for the company's downfall. Taking the culinary world by storm had been his idea, yes, and that gave him more drive to succeed than the rest.

Smirking at the astonished look on his father's face, Finn snatched his notebook and didn't bother to wait for the formality of signing off as he strode away. He heard Gabriel sniggering under his breath, and it took a huge amount of composure for Finn to keep his head high, call the elevator, and wait patiently.

All Finn wanted to do was go back in and punch the smirk off the asshole's face.

THE REST of the workday was blissful compared to that meeting, mostly because Gabriel had the sense not to show his face again.

After reconvening with the engineering team to oversee a patch for a bug that had been crashing the site, Finn sat in his office and used pencils to literally drum up ideas on a notepad. He was confident he could garner the interest of new investors. He didn't need fancy speeches or crazy ideals; he needed some fresh talent to push the idea of sustainability. It had to be someone original and innovative.

How hard could that be to find in New York, of all places?

The subway was unexpectedly empty; the lack of passengers made Finn wonder if there might be a Mardi Gras he was missing or something. When he got home, he went to scrub off the day. His new apartment had some handy automation features, and while he wasn't keen on most of the gimmicks, it was neat that he could program his shower to be running for him when he returned.

He was relishing the scorching water that embraced his carefully maintained figure when he felt the air change. It was charged, somehow, and while the effect was subtle, he knew exactly what it meant.

Stepping out of the shower, Finn was hyperaware of his surroundings. Just like before, every fiber of his being told him to ignore the rising sense of panic, but on reflex, he glanced at the fogged-up mirror in his peripheral vision.

Don't be shy, sexy :)

A chill ran up his spine. This message took the creep factor up a level. It was one thing for a man who'd been raised on the core principles of science to accept being haunted… but since when did ghosts get sexual?

Finn wrapped a towel around his waist and abandoned his shower to check for forced entry for the fifth time that week. There wasn't a single Chinese ornament out of place in his hallway, and not one of the overpriced Van Gogh reproductions had been lifted.

When he returned to the bathroom, he stared at a second line of text written beneath the first.

Drop the towel? ;)

This shit was for real, and what freaked him out the most was that he had no idea what to do. The only logical way for Finn to clear his mind was a hardcore workout. Maybe the harder he worked… the easier his brain could figure it out.

Since his apartment was apparently off-limits, he threw on some clothes and ran down the stairs to get out onto the street. The public gym wouldn't be half as comfortable as his personal one… but maybe the company of ordinary strangers would help.

With no options left, Finn would try anything to get things back to normal.

CHAPTER TWO

TO AN observer, the palm of Jasper's hand laid flat against the invisible barrier at his window was nothing more than an illusion. It had been twelve weeks since he traded the sun-drenched beaches of Rhode Island for the frost-covered spires of the Big Apple, and, courtesy of an unexplainable entrapment, Jasper Wight had spent more time inside his apartment than out of it.

Even if he pressed his full weight against the imperceptible blockade at his door or windows, there was no give. A tangible yet unseen wall of stone only served to cause him pain when he beat at it with his fists.

Jasper couldn't step a single toe out of his door, put his nose out of the window, or even poke a pinky into the gaping hole in the bathroom ceiling.

He'd even tried peeing out of the window once in a particularly desperate moment at three in the morning, but the result was the same as if he'd pissed on a brick wall, and the splash back sanctioned the destruction of what had already been a pitiful carpet. There was no chance he'd get back his security deposit.

Gazing out at all the New Yorkers going about their normal, everyday lives, Jasper's focus drifted, and a vivid memory took center stage.

It was midmorning on a particularly busy Tuesday shift, and when the staircase creaked, alerting Jasper to someone's presence, he swung his legs off the footstool and hopped from his seat.

"Hey, Jas!" Lauren called, the top of her blue hairnet bobbing at the window. "I'm running low on brioche and cinnamon pinwheels!"

"Coming right up!" Jasper called back, throwing out a dusting of flour in case she came in. Over the hum of the oven, his colleague creaked her way back down, and he dove into the fridge to get the dough.

The expanse of his metal workstation was always spotless, and while every utensil had been purposefully laid out to further the façade, most of the appliances were merely for show. The tools would probably be left to gather dust were he not so compulsively tidy; Jasper's greatest instruments were his hands and the power he could channel through them. He only had to cut up the dough with a pizza roller and hover his hands above it before a toasty pulse surged through his skin.

In a matter of seconds, a batch of sweet bread and twenty-four pastries crackled into existence, perfuming the room with a delicious buttery smell.

Taking an empty tray from the head-high stack, he secured the food into the dumbwaiter and buzzed it down. Then he climbed back on his seat and reopened issue number forty-two of *The Oil Painter's Pocketbook*.

The latest edition of his magazine had a section on linseed varnish, and he had longed to try it for some time. But money was tighter than ever since he'd moved to the city, and the minimum wage he made didn't compare to the premium rate he'd earned back in Providence. Still. It had been worth its weight in gold to have that galley kitchen all to himself. That had been his only employment stipulation when he made the bold move across state lines—to work alone and unencumbered.

At first his colleagues couldn't comprehend how he produced the entire menu so quickly, but they let him work in peace when he showed results. If anyone bothered to check the meters, they'd see that since he was hired, the oven and fridge had been dialed down to the lowest setting, and he'd never even switched on the fat fryers.

It would likely be another five or ten minutes before Lauren needed anything else, and since it was almost lunchtime, he swiped some leftover dough and held it in the palm of his hand. The action was so second-nature that he didn't need to tear his gaze away from the magazine to feel the croissant materialize.

Though he had an unlimited repertoire of foodstuffs to craft from thin air, Jasper knew he'd never tire of the classics. He only had to read a recipe once to will anything new into existence, but damn, the Austrians knew what they were doing when they created the first widely known pastries.

Jasper wasn't about to fuck with a good thing.

"More bagels, please!"

Surprised at how well his food was selling, Jasper climbed down from the stool again and dog-eared the page "How to Perfect the Oil Paint Brushstroke." He couldn't wait to get home and practice.

"Sure thing!" he called. "I'm on it!"

ROLLING A completely different piece of dough in his hand, Jasper was reluctant to snap out of his daydream. It had been just under three months since his last shift at the café, and those were better times. Now, as he sat at the window, with the city breeze biting at his face and pigeons cooing their daily song, he'd be lucky to even catch the smell of baked goods over pungent weed and stale piss.

There seemed to be no end to his snare, and he'd come close to giving up trying to bust out when every day began with the same monotonous routine—wake up on a threadbare mattress, remember it wasn't all a dream, fix a strong coffee, and press up against the window to get a physical reminder of the outside world… only to have bastard pigeons snicker at him.

In the twenty-seven years he'd spent on this planet, Jasper never imagined himself ever being jealous of feathered rats.

Some days he'd force himself to study the dozens of arcane tomes on his bookshelf in the hope of discovering an answer. Deciphering the root of the entrapment was taxing, and he'd almost always gravitate toward something else. He even managed to vaguely master astral projection during the forced unemployment.

Being able to manipulate the properties of food could never stack up to the likes of mind control or teleportation… but working alone in the galley kitchen of the café had been the first time in his life he wasn't ridiculed for his unimpressive mage-born gift—mostly because nobody ever actually saw him cast the spells.

That job had been a blissful two weeks, but Jasper had pennies to his name.

Mikasa and Elijah were the only friends he'd made since moving, and as they could apparently come and go as they pleased, he was grateful for their frequent visits and even more grateful that they were temporarily subsidizing his rent. It was unlikely he'd still be on Earth's plane if not for the sympathetic mages who brought him food and company when too much takeout threatened to up a belt notch. Where he could've probably used his abilities to sustain himself… it never had the same sense of achievement when Jasper morphed dinner leftovers versus real produce.

At least he no longer had to endure sweaty sixteen-hour services in the restaurants back in Providence. Being trapped wasn't quite as demoralizing as getting zero credit from the temperamental head chefs when they earned Michelin stars and didn't send so much as a *thank-you* his way. He knew he never got the credit he deserved because he was forbidden by law to perform spells around humans. His mother would have a field day if she had something legitimate to blame his ineptitude on.

Jasper's apartment was so small he didn't have space for a TV even if he could've afforded one. And he almost forgot streaming existed. His cell phone was so old the only means of entertainment was Snake, and he'd spent days on end chomping pixels and avoiding his tail, only to be rewarded with an infuriating Russian hoax.

A lack of gadgets might've bothered some, but not Jasper. Spying on people had become his favorite pastime, and the south-facing bay window was about the only benefit of his overpriced studio. It was both big enough to watch the world below and the perfect angle to create a visual soap opera of his neighbors. He'd have gone stir-crazy if his friends hadn't donated art supplies, and over his months of nonstop painting, the raunchy soap opera spanned the length of twenty-three canvases.

The original plan was to wait for summer, offer his art up to a gallery, and see how the chips fell. Now that summer was almost over, the crucial tourism window was closing, and already he'd missed three of the city's entry-level art shows as a result of some dumb higher power fucking with him. Yet he kept at his work; his imagination ran wild characterizing those he spied on.

When the snare was sprung, and he'd stopped turning his place upside down for an escape, he tried practicing projection to reach out for help. But the task was difficult for even the most practiced mage. His form was always too ethereal and useless. So he'd taken to embodying all of his neighbors' likenesses on canvas instead. It was great fun to capture the beary daddy with a cane in hand, all strict and demanding with the nerdy pizza guy, or to paint the bone-thin twinky boy-next-door type who'd pout in the front-facing camera of his phone, only to spend an hour applying various filters.

It didn't matter what they did. Visual art was Jasper's rawest form of expression, and he tried not to judge his subjects much.

A total of forty canvases already lined the living room. The newest twenty-three were mixed in with the finished pieces he'd brought with him while others were half complete and waiting on the next wave of inspiration. He missed Little Rhody, not just for its sprawling trees and clean air, but also for its "fair value for money per square inch" apartments. He could've had over a hundred pieces safely drying were he still back in Providence.

His motivation had suffered from ogling at the same people all the time, but he got extra incentive when a new tenant moved into the stately penthouse opposite. Because the buildings were close together, Jasper only had to crane his neck to watch as the wizened old lady was replaced by a tall business hunk with a flawless blond pompadour fade. While he was the exact type as every guy his mom had tried to set him up with in the past, he was undeniably hot.

Jasper's crotch had stirred the moment he laid eyes on the dude, and with his carefully sculpted physique, there was no question that he had to paint him in the buff.

His latest piece was almost finished, and as it turned out, spying on Muscles served to improve both Jasper's sexual appetite and his psychological health. Though it hurt his neck to maintain the position for too long, it was handy that the guy had set up his at-home gym along the great expanse of his sheet window, and he seemed to love gazing out at the city during his ritual pre- and post-work sessions. Whatever the reason, Jasper thanked him for it, and the halfway done nude portrait of him midswing on an elliptical was quickly becoming his favorite.

The question of the man's sexual preferences was a brief one. It was obvious by the way his place was always immaculate and how hard he worked to maintain his figure to a stereotypical level. But it was officially confirmed when, at the start of Pride month, he proudly hung a rainbow flag and sang along to Madonna.

Jasper had only the power of imagination for the lower half of the painting. No thanks to the angle of his view, and no matter how hard he tried, his astral visits were never timed well enough for a proper eyeful. A guy with all that confidence must have something to back it up… so he'd been very generous with the brush.

"Jasper?" A muffled yet haughty voice announced itself, sending a bolt of surprise up Jasper's spine. "Why am I looking at a wall? Turn me around this instant!"

"Shit," Jasper whispered as he tossed the dough ball onto the kitchen counter. "Gimme a sec!"

Muffled impatience spurred him on as he shoved cavasses aside to get to the mirror. When he turned it around, his mother's form stared at him with glassy eyes, suspicion plain with the arch of a penciled-in brow.

She wore one of her classic cream blazers, and there wasn't a hair out of place in her razor-sharp bob.

"And where were you last night?" she asked, glaring. "Did a wolf drag you through hell? I was categorically miffed to hear you were a no-show."

He perched the mirror on the counter and raked a hand through the curls of his shoulder-length hair. Since his mom was taking up most of the frame, the reflective portion of the mirror was rendered useless. Jasper grabbed a hairband and tied his hair into a loose bun by feel before he considered the exasperated woman in front of him.

"What do you mean?" he finally asked her.

"It's a simple question, is it not?" She shook her head as she looked off in another direction. Even when they lived in the same state, contact with her had always been staggered at best. "I had yet another suitor arranged for you, but he said you failed to turn up."

"Mom," Jasper said, "I've been in New York for over three months now. I haven't been to that snooty restaurant since I broke it off with the last one. Blayze, was it? What a dumbass name."

Irritation flitted across her face, but it was gone in a flash, a false smile in its stead. "Oh, right. Now I remember. Moving there was never a permanent solution, though, was it? Just another one of your fads."

"Is that so?" Jasper scowled and bit back a retort. All his family were powerful mages with great influence, and his mom had a tedious, desperate desire for him to stand out in their hidden society. "Regardless of that, something terrible has happened. I've somehow managed to trap myse—"

"Honestly, Jasper. I don't want to hear more excuses. Get your priorities in order and stop trying to humiliate me."

"I'm not. And I have to tell yo—"

"If you don't start pulling your weight, your father and I will—well, I don't exactly know *what* we'll do. But… we will. Anyway, I must dash. Your sister has changed the seating arrangement for the wedding for the fourth time." He could see his mom had already mentally checked out, too busy thinking about her next plan. "And for God's sake, get a haircut."

"Mom, I *really* need to tell you somethi—"

Too late. Before he could so much as mention entrapment, the mirror was back to normal and showed only the dumfounded lines engraved on Jasper's face.

"Shit," he breathed, wishing for the hundredth time he knew the incantation to dial out. This was one of those moments he wished he'd spent more time paying attention in school and less time staring at guys' asses.

JASPER WAS pissy after the impromptu mirror-call from his mom, so much so that even painting couldn't lift his mood. He was too angry to finish his lusty magnum opus, too restless to start something new. He resigned himself to pacing the apartment and trying to unravel his thoughts.

The fact his mom didn't know her son had crossed state lines months ago wasn't all that bad. She was always wrapped up with work. No, the thing that pissed him off was that she didn't know, or if she did, she didn't care that his sister hadn't invited him to her wedding.

As kids, Sara was the golden child in every sense of the word. These days she was too busy making seven figures in Dallas from her innate gift of cajolery to care about anyone but herself. Money was all anyone cared about these days—that and power. His mom could use tranquility at will, and the mask of compassion she donned among humans earned her a senior role within the US Supreme Court. And Christ knew what his dad got up to in his spare time with his affinity for pyrotechnics.

He did have one thing in common with other mages, though—cluelessness. Nobody knew how, when, or why their talents came to be, but everyone had long since given up asking. Now it was simply a truth kept from human knowledge at all costs. Perhaps Jasper was God's conduit to make better-tasting food. Perhaps he was the answer to world hunger. Who knew? Not Jasper. He didn't much care for the politics of circumstance.

The only thing he really cared about was the logistics of his *current* circumstance. He felt more cooped up than a battery hen, and he ached to rejoin the world. There had to be a way, something he was neglecting to understand.

It had all been fun and games when he first projected into the guy's apartment and left messages on the fancy steamed-up mirror. They were playful and innocent, but the little taste of freedom made

Jasper more determined to escape with each passing day. The talk with his mom had tipped the scales further, and now the need to escape wasn't just because boredom was an ever-present dog on his heels. The dose of life-affirming motivation he'd received after seeing Muscles so at ease with his freedom fanned the flames of his yearning to rejoin the world.

Perhaps today was high time to push the boundaries.

Sitting cross-legged on the floor, Jasper emptied his mind. He focused on the raw energy that made him able to channel his day-to-day spells. It was more like sensing a color than feeling something physical—a kind of purplish fog he latched on to with his mind's eye and let encompass him.

Before long, a thousand points tingled across his flesh, and his reality dissolved into ferocious vibration. Next thing he knew, his very essence was transported a hundred feet across the street, just as he desired, and right into the heart of the spotless apartment for the sixth time that week.

Rising with the grace of a fallen angel, Jasper's movements were compensated by the fact that his vision was slightly askew, blurred as though he'd removed a pair of contacts.

Because Muscles always vacated the property at 8:00 a.m. sharp and returned at 7:30 p.m. on the dot, he shouldn't have been surprised to hear the shower running on its own or find the guy walking through the door. But it was always a refreshing surprise to see the actuality of his imposing stature.

After the man dropped his keys into an ornate bowl, he walked right up to where Jasper was hovering, and a bolt of shock tore through the mage's core. Could the man see him? Had he screwed up the spell somehow?

No. The man's jade eyes were fixed in his direction, but he walked right through Jasper's form to reach the window and puffed a sigh as he gazed at the city.

Jasper probably would've blushed if it were possible. He probably should've felt bad for the intrusion, but he'd grown up around family who didn't know the meaning of personal space. He was sure the guy would see the fun side of it. And it wasn't like he had much choice.

Previous visiting attempts with others had been laughable. It wasn't until further study on astral projection that he learned he wasn't able to physically manifest or even interact with objects until he felt a connection with the recipient.

He'd felt that connection with Muscles the moment he laid eyes on him.

The man grabbed a decanter from a side table, fixed himself a generous measure of whiskey, and whipped a top-shelf cell phone from his pants pocket. Jasper floated above the carpet, keeping a tentative distance as the man punched a number on speed dial and held the device to his ear.

"Hey," Muscles said, tone curt as he swigged his drink. "You weren't supposed to call until later on this month."

The guy's brow furrowed as he listened to the response. Jasper leaned in to try to catch the recipient's voice, but he remembered it was useless. Technology and magic don't mix. He'd found that out on past visits when the guy would switch on the television and pore over files, then pump iron in his private gym, and finally cook up a juicy steak and sip chardonnay. Jasper could never see what programs he liked to watch or what he browsed through on his phone. Other nights, the man would have a longer shower, drink a big glass of whiskey, and put a blanket over his lap while scrolling through an iPad. Again, his intentions were inferable... but unclear.

Whenever Jasper navigated through the astral plane, images on devices were replaced with static. He was certain the guy was using hookup apps, and with the influx of men who visited and downloaded apps during Pride month, he'd have the pick of the litter. But Jasper could never see the type of person Muscles tried for or what porn he touched himself to.

Frankly, it was starting to piss him off.

"I *realize* that," Muscles continued, almost finished with his whiskey. "If you can give me another month, I'll prove what I'm capable of."

Was he talking to a relative or a colleague? His words remained clipped over the course of the conversation until he snapped his cell shut and drained his glass. Whoever it was couldn't be in the picture very much.

It seemed Muscles was even more solitary than Jasper. Given his clothes, apartment, and long days, he had to be another rich highflier whose problems were inconsequential to the meek. Pretty much the poster child of every man Jasper's mom had ever set him up with, even though he always turned them down.

At first, that had made Muscles fun to fuck with. Then his crotch stirred at the thought of painting him nude because, try as he might, Jasper couldn't deny his level of sexiness. He ached to touch the unobtainable man.

Since Muscles was prepping for his next shower, Jasper readied himself to write another message. He wondered what the guy did on weekends while he vacated the place for hours on end. What might he do when he wasn't so consumed by work? Doubtless he was the type who could never switch off. He was sturdy. Just by the tight set of his shoulders, Jasper knew the guy took life too seriously.

At the sink Jasper forced his eyes closed and waited to hear the click of the shower door. The mirror was already steamed up, so he set to work.

It had to be more direct this time. The other notes had been too gentle and playful, what with the hashtags. Now he was more anxious than ever to get a reply.

'I need help, please respo—'

The guy had stepped out of the shower too soon, so the plea was cut short, leaving a squiggly finger-trail in the condensation. Muscles had predicted Jasper's arrival, and there was no longer disbelief written on his face. It looked like a bizarre version of acceptance.

This is it. Now or never.

It was a test of Jasper's willpower to gather all of his knowledge and thrust his magical limits. When he felt a scratchy kind of change wash over him, the floor solidified beneath his feet. He had been successful, and Muscles was turning his head in a painful slo-mo.

"Hello…." Jasper's voice was garbled because his mouth didn't technically exist and he'd never bothered to practice sound projection. "I'm Jasper."

A brand-new expression crossed the man's gorgeously dimpled face. Shock? No doubt. Something else too.

Time ran out. Before Jasper could speak, the man stuck a hand through his body and then ran for the hills when it passed right through.

Muscles had left the towel behind in his haste, and as Jasper prepared to return to his body, he couldn't contain his grin. The eyeful he'd been so hoping for had been right in front of him, and he'd been spot-on to add those extra inches in the painting.

Returning to his body had never been so bittersweet. Jasper wasn't happy to be back in his shitty little place, but the image of Muscles's toned ass would undoubtedly help him pass the rest of the night.

CHAPTER THREE

FINN THREW on some streetwear and slammed the door of his apartment shut as he bolted from the room. He was tempted to turn the winding stairs into a Slip 'N Slide to get out of the building faster but settled on running his sweaty palms along the handrails, taking three steps at a time.

He couldn't rationalize what had just happened. It was too crazy. Ghosts are supposed to be ugly, sheet-wearing things. Not half-naked, stupidly attractive young men. Finn shook his head as the mere memory made his crotch stir.

He'd seen a variety of holograms when he attended a Tokyo VR expo last year. The company was a pioneer in simulations and cybernetics, and though it was impressive to see the lead cast of *Sailor Moon* twirl around and twiddle their hair for lonely fanboys, it was easy to tell the difference between human and decoy. Especially as the emitters made a distinctive buzz.

So… what the fuck was that back there? Whatever was standing in the bathroom was something entirely different—neither real nor fake. No obviously scripted movements, no generic projection hum. The only explanation for it was implausible. Unbelievable.

It threatened to break his scientific brain.

The streets outside weren't offering much solace either. Striding through Times Square, at least a hundred electric billboards tried to grab his attention. Even in daylight it was hard to ignore all the ad campaigns, and in the back of his head, Finn dreamed *Zest* would have pride of place one day.

As he surveyed throngs of people shuffling around the gloomy twilight, Finn realized he didn't have much of a plan. He bet he looked like shit. He sure felt like it.

Coffee. A strong Americano was his best chance to allow his mind to unravel. Luckily the economic answer to his generation's caffeine addiction was to put at least four baristas on every block.

Heading to his favorite independent café on 54th Street, Finn tried preening himself in shop windows. He was neither subtle nor successful. Without a chance to use his freeze-hold hairspray, it wasn't long before his blond waves became stringy and tickled his forehead. The sweatpants he'd thrown on were already saturated with moisture in the worst places, and his face was gaunt. He looked like a hobo—a hobo who'd literally seen a ghost.

Thankfully the coffeehouse was mostly vacant, and the smell of roasted beans roused Finn's senses as he stepped up to order.

When a young couple handed over cash for iced lattes then linked arms before heading out into the early evening, Finn was surprised to find himself watching them intently. Though he was a self-proclaimed loner, he envied their togetherness.

"What can I get for you, sir?"

The barista, Danielle, utilized a schooled politeness by offering him a sweet smile. Finn wondered if she called him *sir* because he was at least a decade older than her. Or was it because she was used to seeing him wrapped up in a suit when he dashed in here every day? He wondered why he even cared.

"Tall Americano with hot milk." Finn almost forgot to specify that he wasn't rushed for time. "For here, please."

"Coming right up!" The sugary smile was back, but it was wasted on Finn. His mind was halfway through a 5K sprint.

He gazed at the replica Egyptian tapestry covering the walls. It served as a welcome distraction, since he knew it would take a mental toll to sit down and mull over the last half hour. He still wasn't ready and he'd never studied the intricate scenes decorated on the woven fabric.

And yet, Danielle was ready. She had his drink prepared in record-breaking time. Between the artwork and the questions buzzing around his head, it had been too easy to get lost.

"Thanks," said Finn. He forked over a Hamilton and didn't bother to wait for change.

When he carried his tray over to a table near the window, he sat with his back to everyone and sipped on the caffeinated lava.

As he surveyed the bright bustling outside, his hands trembled around the mug as he tried to comprehend it all.

Was he finally losing his mind? All his college friends had told him he fixated on stuff too often. Maybe another visit to Dr. Nash was due. *Jesus.* He hadn't seen the therapist in eight years, and he would have dollar signs in his eyes the moment Finn called. It would take all of two minutes for the professional persuader to rope him into a new string of sessions that would be an even bigger drain on his mental stamina. Not exactly what Finn needed when everything was already up in the air at work.

The sound of laughter broke his reverie. Finn was in an unusually bitter mood, and it struck him as odd for people to act so gaily when he was at his worst. He needed friends. Where did normal people look for things like that?

He looked around the room and wondered if fate was on his side. Elderly couples were reading newspapers, and parties of one were typing up playscripts on their Macs. Only a handful were entertaining face-to-face interactions. Even then, how would Finn randomly interject himself in a way that didn't make him seem like a total nut job?

When he landed on a couple seated just a little farther along the window, his gaze lingered. A nimble lady with flawless chocolate skin and fiery red hair sat next to a broad guy who had an electric-blue mane. Both nursed coffee mugs and were dressed head to toe in black, mostly leather. Not unusual, especially not if these guys were native New Yorkers, but both hairdos were strikingly glossy beneath the dim lighting, and there was something different about them.

"He told me the guy almost had a heart attack after the first message," said the redhead, voice all husky and mysterious. "That he ran out of the house naked."

"Really?" asked her companion, the bold lines of his face creasing with mirth. "I'd have been a lot more direct in his position. Stood my ground and told him what's what."

Finn sipped his drink, trying to steer his attention elsewhere, but curiosity got the better of him quicker than he expected, and when he gave the pair another glance, he blanched. He knew what was wrong with them. Why they were different from everyone else.

They looked at bit like the ghost guy. It was no coincidence.

When Finn pictured the spectral entity, he was shocked to realize that he had been cute in a weird, endearing kind of way. And he had also been smiling in what might've been an attempt to lessen the blow of his arrival. These people had some kind of mark on the side of their necks, and Finn's ghost had had one too, though Finn had only just recollected it. Where the girl had a brain, and the guy had a branch, his ghost had worn a very questionable mark—maybe a donut or a misshapen croissant—definitely something food related.

Finn caught himself drifting. He sipped his drink and tried to steer his attention elsewhere and focus on anything other than snooping. A random stack of magazines at the side seemed like a good time killer, and he considered picking one up, but then his heart sank. He'd spotted three culinary mags, and he couldn't find any of the old issues belonging to his company. They should be placed at the top. Actually, fuck that. They should be sold over the counter.

"I feel *so* bad for him," the woman continued, reeling Finn right back in. "Trapped indefinitely like that, reaching out to strangers for help."

"Me too," the guy said. "Though I hear the guy he's haunting is *super* freaking hot. Like, Christian Bale hot. So, it can't be all that bad."

Finn stopped drinking midsip. Their conversation was sounding familiar somehow. Haunting? Trapped and reaching out for help? Was that what Finn's ghost had been trying to do?

When part of a jigsaw clicked together in Finn's head, ice ran through his veins.

All of it was linked. They knew him, what he'd been doing. Probably were walking ghosts, just like him.

He stared into his foam-laden mug for answers. Maybe they were all in on this together. Why else would they be here talking so openly? To set him up for a trap of some kind?

Now that they'd finished their drinks, they were getting up to leave. Finn had to decide. To follow or not to follow?

This was crazy behavior. Those people were keeping to themselves, probably keen to just go about their day. It was almost impossible that they were involved in Finn's life.

And yet… stranger things had happened.

Who was he kidding? Finn felt a surge of energy when he downed the dregs of his coffee and jumped off the stool. He had no choice but to follow them.

FINN HAD seen enough cop shows to feel confident of his stealth abilities, especially now that the snow was getting deeper and the evenings were getting longer. The earlier dusk meant the nonstop stream of tourists was thick enough to make good cover as he tailed the couple.

That didn't necessarily mean he felt good about the snap decision. It wasn't like him to act on such a weird impulse, but the pair had seemed odd even before he saw the marks on their necks. That was just the final straw. Finn craved an answer to his bizarre circumstances, and they might very well have the key.

"Watch out, bud!" a big beefy guy said when Finn bumped into his shoulder.

"Sorry," he said in passing, fixed on the couple.

They were walking hand in hand, and there were too many people in front to make out what was so funny that had both of them in tears. Odd. They hadn't seemed like a couple before.

He wondered what Ghost Guy had been trying to accomplish by scaring him. Taunting him? Maybe it was all Gabriel's idea to rile him up. Or was it all the handiwork of the people he was tailing? Either way, he knew he wasn't crazy, because they were heading straight toward Finn's apartment.

He imagined himself following them right up to the door, jumping out and surprising them. And yet, when they dodged taxis to cross the road, they went into the apartment house opposite, and Finn began to question his sanity again.

It was decision time once more. He'd already come this far. Might as well see it through. He had no other leads, and he was anxious to get shit sorted.

Staring at his watch to count down a full minute, Finn crossed the street and followed them in. This building wasn't even a fifth as swanky as his, so there was no front desk or keycards needed to gain entrance to the revolving doors, and he saw the backs of their very distinct heads getting into an elevator.

There was, however, a janitor mopping the tiled floors, and he gave a sharp side-eye as Finn went up to the elevator and stared at the electronic panel rather than pressing the call button. On the blinking information screen, their apparent destination was the thirteenth floor. *Fitting.*

Finn had no time to lose, and he already knew he'd forgo the night's workout session when he bolted up the winding staircase. He had to get there before the elevator did if he wanted to finish the chase, and he was quicker than a bat out of hell as he took three steps at a time.

He started seeing spots after floor number eleven. When Finn reached the top, he dashed over to the side and let out a sigh of relief as the elevator pinged shut, having just deposited its cargo. His prey sauntered down the corridor, none the wiser to his snooping.

Finn took some measured breaths and continued.

The pair were still laughing and chatting, but from what he could hear, their conversation wasn't pertinent anymore. Making sure to stay hidden as they rounded the labyrinth of apartments, Finn followed as innocently as possible.

When they came to door number 137B, the redhead took out a set of keys and held the door open for her friend and closed the door behind them. The volume of chatter rose above the din of some busted air conditioner, and Finn took time to assess his situation.

This wasn't normal behavior. He got that. But neither was trying to fuck up someone's life with stupid messages and fake projections. Or real projections. Whatever they were, it had to stop so he could focus on work and get back to real life.

Finn didn't have a plan as he walked up to the door and pounded a fist on it. He was sure he'd come up with something to say, some reason as to why a total stranger had followed the pair home. They were the key to getting his life back on track. They knew something, and he had to act boldly.

All of that went to shit when the door swung open. The ghost had answered, in the flesh, right in front of Finn's face.

His look of surprise twinned the one that Finn now wore, and the people he'd stalked had huge, expectant grins on their faces as they perched on a patchwork couch.

"Holy crap," Ghost blurted out.

He knew it must be the same voice… just more genuine. Earlier it sounded like it was coming from the bottom of a glass jar—distorted and edged with resonance. Now it was crisp and buttery smooth. It confused Finn that much more.

"Well, umm," Finn ventured, motionless, utterly dumfounded. "Hi?"

"I…." The crease deepened across Ghost's brow. "Um… I guess you'd better come in."

CHAPTER FOUR

JASPER HAD no idea what Muscles was doing at his door, but there was no question whether or not to let him in. It was fate, and he wasn't about to piss off the universe any more than he apparently already had.

The guy was hesitant. Perhaps even reluctant. The abhorrent look of astonishment wasn't leaving his gorgeously carved face.

"It's all right," Jasper said, shrugging. "My friends can just… leave?"

He tried acting casual as he threw a sharp glance toward Mikasa and Elijah, but he was closer to shitting himself. He had no idea how the dreamboat was here, let alone why. But he recognized smugness— his friends were in on it.

"What have you guys don–"

"You're welcome," Elijah said as they rose from the couch in unison.

"You were right, Jas," said Mikasa before patting his shoulder. "He *is* gorgeous."

"Go on in. He doesn't bite." Elijah squeezed past Muscles, still caught on the threshold. "Too hard, anyway."

The sound of their giggling echoed throughout the corridor as they went toward the elevator.

"Those conniving bastards," Jasper muttered. He should've known something was up the moment they arrived. He'd never seen Mikasa so quiet. She always had something amusing to say about human politics or one of her latest hookups.

"Did they know I'd been following them?" The man's self-assured voice sent a shiver down Jasper's spine, and he suppressed the urge to melt.

"More than likely." Jasper gave Muscles another shrug and paired it with a tentative smile. "Wanna talk about *why* you did? Or do you make a habit of tailing people?"

The pin was back in the tension grenade when he finally stepped in. Then Jasper remembered his latest painting, and as the guy closed the door, he scrambled to throw a scrap of blue tarp over it.

Nervous laughter followed, and Jasper put his hands in his pockets.

"So…." Muscles caved first. "You're the ghost who's been haunting me?"

Jasper burst out with an ugly hoot, then shoved a fist in his mouth to stop himself.

Was this guy serious? "You thought I was a ghost?"

Muscles tilted his head and stared. "Well, yeah. You've been appearing in my apartment to write messages on my mirror for the past week, haven't you?"

Jasper tried not to shrug again and felt his cheeks grow hot instead. He had to get hold of himself.

"Yeah," Jasper said casually, moving to his kitchen island to fix a strong cup of coffee. He'd already had five, but he needed another. He held up a floral bone-china mug. "Would you like one?"

"Just had one," Muscles said, eyeing the grime-ridden floor, "but, sure, why not?"

As the Adonis surveyed the open-plan room, a different kind of heat rose in Jasper's cheeks. The place was a shithole, and he wished his first meeting with this walking god weren't where he'd been festering for months on end. He'd have to find a way to spray some air freshener without drawing too much attention.

"Though, do you maybe have anything stronger?"

"Sure," Jasper said, reaching to get some whiskey out of the bottom cupboard. It was cheap, nasty stuff, nothing like the single malt he'd seen Muscles sipping. He didn't mention that part yet. It was better to let him breathe and digest this not-so chance meeting.

He was half-surprised he hadn't already fired a hundred questions. "If I'm pouring you a drink, do I finally get to learn your name?"

"Oh… uh, yeah." The guy was nervous. It was easy to see by the way he kept putting his hands in his pockets and taking them out just to rake them through the bleached curls of that sexy pompadour fade. "It's Finn. My name's Finn."

Jasper bobbed his head in acknowledgment and smiled as he topped off the tumbler.

"Pleasure to meet you, Finn. I'm Jasper." He cursed himself for sounding so robotic. Why was he acting like a Boy Scout about to get his first medal?

Finn cocked an eyebrow, evidently unsure whether to look pleased or alarmed. "Jasper? Like, as in, Casper the Friendly Ghost?"

"Well, it sounds silly when you put it like that. But yeah. It's good to meet you in person, Finn." As he walked around the island, Jasper passed Finn the drink and prolonged the skin-on-skin contact for longer than necessary. It didn't go unnoticed. There was plain recognition in Finn's eyes at the motive, and their gazes remained locked for a few seconds. Then he looked at the damned floor again.

"How long have you been doing—" Finn gestured aimlessly with his tumbler. "—whatever it is you've been doing?"

Jasper sighed as he prepped his coffee. "With you? Just the week since you moved in."

Something caught in Finn's throat. It sounded like disapproval, but he was quick to cover up the frown with a forced laugh. "You've done this to others as well?"

"For a few months, yeah." Jasper stumbled over the words, still nervous. "I'm, er. I'm not very good at it."

Over the brim of his steaming cup, Jasper eyed Finn's reaction. Now that his nerves were beginning to settle, he was visibly more confident.

Jasper went to the couch and pushed aside the painting debris. "What I mean to say is, I was never successful in manifesting my projections with anyone but you."

"And what does that mean, exactly?" Finn looked eager to understand, and it was plain it took a lot of effort for him to stand still and figure it out. "Are you some kind of…." He eyed the collection of arcane tomes scattered on the small desk and lining the bookcase. "Some kind of… wizard?"

"You could say that," Jasper chuckled. "Though it's not what we like to call ourselves. Not if we're being socially correct, I mean. It conjures images of wands, brooms, and cauldrons. We don't all run around with scars and broken glasses." Jasper's jovial tone fizzled out, and he breathed deeply when he didn't get the desired response. "I've been trapped here for almost three months now, and because it's frankly been boring me to tears, I reached out for help the day you moved in. Couldn't help myself."

"Trapped?" Finn repeated, scowl deepening. "Like, as in, you can't leave?"

"Pretty much." Jasper searched Finn's face for reproach, but there was nothing except the willingness to understand. It was commendable given the circumstances. "Look."

Jasper went to the window where he'd spent weeks spying on his neighbors. When he cracked the hinge of his only place of inspiration, cold air flew in. Yet when he tried to reach out, his index finger met the invisible barrier just as he knew it would.

When he pushed hard, Finn gasped behind him.

Jasper was shoving with all his might at an angle that should have pitched him out the window and onto the fire escape just beyond. But that didn't happen.

"The fuck?" Finn got up, compelled to investigate.

He gazed at the invisible barrier and examined it to see if there was some kind of hidden trick. It was clear Jasper was pressing with all his might and there was still no give. When Finn stuck out his own hand, it went all the way, just as expected.

It was one thing to know Finn was perfectly free; another thing altogether to watch him thrust his arm in and out the window as he attempted to find the source of Jasper's apparent trick. It was like torture, but Jasper sensed no malice in it.

"And this," Jasper said, enjoying the look on Finn's face as he went to the front door, opened it, rammed himself outrageously into the invisible barrier, and rebounded onto his backside.

"That's *so* fucked," Finn said. He waved a tentative hand across the threshold, clearly afraid to also wind up trapped.

When it passed through without fuss, Finn stepped through and out of the apartment. He looked back with pity.

"I know," Jasper sighed dramatically and took a seat on the couch. "Don't ask me how or why. Nobody seems able to figure it out."

"Shit," Finn sighed as he softly closed the door. There was a long pause when he came back in, broken only when he took a swig of his drink.

When he went back to the window, Finn looked up at his own apartment. The vantage was less than perfect but good enough to spy.

Finn drained the rest of his drink and held it out for a refill. Jasper was hardly about to deny him.

"Help yourself."

Jasper wasn't planning on getting Finn drunk—though it would make short work of seducing him. He wanted Finn to feel comfortable and at ease during what was a difficult time. It was hard for Jasper too. Telling nonmagical beings about the existence of the mystical was a big fat no-go ingrained in every mage's brain along with their ABCs. Finn was the first human he'd ever broken the rules for.

Jasper would be wading through deep shit right now if anyone found out. But then… Mikasa and Elijah were nothing if not complicit, and they wouldn't have helped break the rules if it weren't such a desperate time.

As he poured the drink, Finn's hands shook so much that he clinked bottle to glass. When Jasper looked at him questioningly, he turned up the corners of his mouth ever so slightly. Though it was weak by anyone's standards, it was the first smile since he'd walked in.

Feeling out of his element, Jasper tried to ground himself. This fateful meeting was too important to allow himself to get sidetracked, but words were failing him. He had no idea how to soften the blow of this crazy info dump.

"Finn...."

"Gah," Finn shouted and spilled whiskey over his lap when the sound of Jasper's voice startled him. "Aw, man, this is gonna leave a stain."

Suppressing a giggle, Jasper got up to fetch him a towel. When Finn began mopping up the spillage, tutting all the while, Jasper had to sit back down and cross his legs to stop the stirring in his crotch.

"You were away with the fairies," said Jasper. "It's all right. I go there too, sometimes."

"Wait." Finn paused his cleaning, voice dipping low. "Don't tell me they're real too? All of this... it's got to be some kind of joke."

"It's just a figure of speech," Jasper said evenly, trying to lighten the mood. What he was saying might be batshit, but Finn wouldn't still be here if he didn't want to listen. Shuffling, Jasper attempted to make space for the big stud on the couch. *Man*, he wished the place weren't such a shithole. "I get why you'd ask, though. This must be a headfuck for sure. I'll try to bear that in mind."

Nodding slowly, seeming to settle a little, Finn peered over his glass. He had a strange habit of lingering his gaze for just a few seconds longer than normal, and Jasper wasn't about to tell him to stop because he relished every millisecond those cool green eyes searched his face. Finn seemed to see beyond the crazy, and the man was everything he could've hoped for and more. After having spied on him for a good while, Jasper felt he already knew the guy inside and out, so it was nothing short of astonishing that the feeling could be reciprocated.

"Well, I'm waiting." Finn crossed one leg over the other and rested the tumbler on his knee. "For an explanation. To all of this. What the hell's been going on?"

"Okay, okay," Jasper said, holding a hand up before he downed his coffee. This was one of the rare times he wished he smoked, and he wasn't about to drink to excess and make a fool of himself in front of his newest crush. "I think it's better if I show you rather than tell you."

NORMALLY, WHEN Jasper projected, he preferred to sit cross-legged on the floor to ground himself to something physical. But he recognized the importance of the moment, and he didn't want to be embarrassed by his abilities, so he tried his hardest to empty his brain of all thoughts and emotion as he sat on the couch—a hard ask considering his mind was sprinting light-years to be cool enough to flirt and because the pent-up sexual tension threatened to tear him apart.

Jasper managed to keep his composure. Using a stored-away reserve of willpower, he focused the purplish haze just as he'd done before, and he was probably as surprised as Finn to see himself climb out of his own body and stand in a projected ethereal silhouette.

"Hi there," Jasper said, giving a wave for lack of any sense of what to do next.

"What the fuck," Finn stated. It wasn't a question, just a perfectly rational reaction as he got up, weaved his way through IKEA's finest space-saving furniture, and put a hand through the form. "Can you feel that?"

"Nope," Jasper said, offering a grin. The blurriness was damn near torture. Having Finn so close and willing to touch… in a sense… made both his fake heart and the real thing pound. Hard.

Finn circled, gazing as though he were an ant struggling to comprehend the scale of the planet. "Why is your voice different? Like all tinny and echoey?"

Jasper shrugged but then remembered to use his words. "Beats me. I've only just learned how to do this."

"How remarkable," Finn mused. "Nobody's going to believe this!"

"Oh, no. You can't tell anyone." Jasper was stern as his eyes snapped open, the words coming from his mouth as his astral form disappeared into the air. There was more surprise on Finn's face, and he looked at the physical Jasper with eyes wider than garbage cans.

Jasper tensed. Would this be the deal breaker?

"Why not?" Finn asked. "This is nothing short of incredible. It could have a thousand different uses in today's world. Delivery service, world travel, espionage—you name it. I bet this could put the human race fifty years ahead of itself."

Jasper still wasn't used to rejoining himself, and it still left him out of sorts. Having roped in the silver cord so swiftly and unintentionally left him feeling slightly nauseated and weirdly craving sugar.

"Remarkable," Finn repeated.

Jasper held up a hand.

Taking a few deep breaths, he wobbled off the couch and went to fetch something sweet from the drawer. A Ding Dong would do nicely this time. "I get low blood sugar after using my abilities."

"How does it all work?" Finn asked. "I mean, have you always been like this? Or is it something anybody can learn with practice?"

"Mages are born, not made or learned," Jasper said. If it came across pompous… so be it. "You can't learn magic any more than you can just *become* a true-born Frenchman. You have to be of mage blood to learn anything in the mystic arts. Sorry."

Finn waved a hand, pretending he wasn't upset by the news, but his body language said otherwise. "So." Finn took a breath. "You're telling me there's millions of people around the world who have powers? Like the X-Men? Or the Avengers?"

"Sure. Except we aren't a band of ragtag rebels with a cause. Most of us have accepted our place in society and aren't planning an uprising. At least, not anytime soon. You guys are safe for now."

"So, it's like those Potter books? Secret Society and all?" Amusement was plain in Finn's tone of voice despite the poor joke.

"Well, no. We each have a different set of abilities. There's a little overlap of power, but not too much."

"Wait a sec. *Most* of you accepted?" Finn asked suddenly, seeming to have only just processed Jasper's words. "What happens to the others? The ones that don't accept it?"

Jasper sighed and turned to Finn, trying to figure out how best to put across details without scaring him or sending him running straight to the cops. "There's a remote island off the coast of Japan where the majority of nonconformists… er… go to live. It's not that they think they're superior, necessarily. Some people just don't enjoy cohabiting with humans in secret because they can never be their true selves."

"Oh… that's fair enough, I guess. Man, this is a lot."

By the crease on his forehead and glazed-over eyes, Jasper had no doubt Finn was picturing the place.

"I don't know the island's name, before you ask. And I wouldn't be allowed to tell you even if I did. I've already gone against mage code by revealing myself, as it is."

To help him understand, Jasper would've painted a visual picture of the island, but he'd only heard a few stories about it. He'd never been and wouldn't need to go. He had no illusions of grandeur, and he was certain he'd be content again if he could just get out of his apartment.

"Well," Finn started, "what happens if there's an outbreak or some kind of incident?"

"In the Magical Regulation Force, there's a guy who can wipe memories with just his voice. There's a few other telepaths and suggesters who can do similar things. Kind of scary, actually."

"No shit!" Sweat was starting to form on Finn's brow. "You're telling me I could've lived an entirely different life and I'd have no memory of it?"

"I suppose so. But their intentions are honest, and the people elected for those jobs would never do that," Jasper insisted. "Whenever there's an incident and something lets loose, they wipe the memories of those affected and send the mage responsible to live on the island."

"An island full of supers…." Finn let that hang in the air for a bit. "I take it I wouldn't be able to just happen across it if I went looking?"

"Nope. It's enchanted, like a fortress surrounded by an invisible barrier that steers away anything manmade."

"Jesus." Finn shook his head. "Are you going to get in a lot of shit for telling me this? What's to stop me running to a reporter when I leave?"

"Other than the fact they would probably laugh you out the door? Not much, I guess. But I don't believe you would do something like that. You're too intrigued."

Finn smiled. Somehow, they both knew he wouldn't do something so foolish, especially not when there was so much more to learn.

"So, can you do anything else?"

Jasper rolled his eyes and chuckled. As though projecting himself out of his body weren't enough. Then he remembered he had a snack cake in his hand, and he had an innate gift he'd known about since age six. Why was he acting like such a damned forgetful fool?

Jasper was impressed at how well Finn was taking all this, so he made one more attempt to show off. Anything to earn his favor.

Placing the half-eaten cake on the counter, he hovered his hands over it and put years of practice to use. Because it was ingrained into his mind, altering the state of foodstuffs was considerably easier than projecting. His intent to turn an ordinary snack cake into a decadent cheesecake was tough but doable, and it took only half a minute to summon a velvety layer of cream cheese to sit on top of a buttery cookie base. There was even a berry coulis on top, striped with mille-feuille-style chevrons.

"Holy. Shit." Finn got up to admire Jasper's handiwork. Beyond further shock and awe, the man's face was unreadable. It looked as if he'd gone a bit pale... but that could've been down to the poor lighting in the apartment.

"Neat, huh?" Jasper asked, fetching a fork from the kitchen and trying to act like his gift wasn't the most useless magical ability on the planet. There was every chance the gorgeous hunk didn't see it like that.

"Uh. Yeah." Finn's gaze was darting about the place. "So, what do you call this gift of yours?"

"The technical term for my gift is transmutation... but I prefer Gastromancer."

"Clever," Finn chuckled. "Is that why you have that tattoo on your neck? What is it, a croissant?"

"This?" Jasper forked a piece, then reached to touch the spot on his neck where he'd gotten inked so long ago that he barely even registered its existence when he looked in the mirror. "It's a loaf of bread that's meant to represent food as a whole. Something about its symbolism being embedded with everyday life or... something. It was Mom's idea to make me feel better about my gift."

When he was done ogling Jasper's mark, Finn looked from the piece of cheesecake and back to Jasper. Raw emotion teemed behind his eyes, and Jasper couldn't decipher what it meant.

Leaning in slowly, Finn opened his mouth as though they were starring roles at the midpoint of a Hollywood rom-com. Just as he was about to take the cake, Jasper handed him the fork instead.

As Finn chewed, Jasper offered an awkward smile.

Finn had gone beet red, and the expression on his face told Jasper everything he needed to know. The cheesecake was clearly divine, and Finn was eyeing it on the sly.

"Well, um, I, er, need to dash," Finn said suddenly. "Got a big day tomorrow."

Jasper wanted to speak, but Finn had turned around and was heading out of the apartment before he could so much as hold a finger up in protest.

"Shit," he muttered to the firmly closed door.

Torn, Jasper had no idea whether he'd succeeded in reassuring Finn by answering his questions… or whether he'd just freaked the shit out of him.

CHAPTER FIVE

As SOON as the door closed, Finn plonked himself down in the hallway and focused on nothing except leveling his breathing.

Seeing Jasper in the flesh had been overwhelming, and beyond the instant attraction, Finn was still processing everything he'd said. Everything he'd claimed. Everything he'd somehow convinced Finn of.

Finn didn't know which was worse—the ludicrous things that had come out of Jasper's mouth or the fact Finn had been so quick to believe all of it. But when somebody says they can do something extraordinary and then they go on to show it and prove it, how could he possibly deny it? Of course… that didn't mean he was comfortable with it.

Magic and fairytales were buried in the past, way back when Finn dreamed of being an actor on Broadway. Now those fantasies had shot from the grave like a vampire decked out in Disney merch. There were possibilities. Excitement.

There was hope, even, but it made his head spin. And this was just the tip of the iceberg.

There was so much more to learn, and half of him wanted to turn and walk right back in. But he recognized the need for space. He'd done well to keep his composure and act casual. Jasper was oddly disarming, but Finn needed time to process before he could even think about going back.

Finn didn't have the energy to walk back down the steps, so he got up and called the elevator. He made the short walk home on autopilot, weaving through tourists. He blocked out their nonsense as he wondered who else in the world was like the handsome mage holed up in his apartment. Who was gifted, and what influence did they have now as they went about their seemingly normal lives? How many were there, and just what were they doing? Had he just walked past one, or was that woman with pigtails in the pink chiffon dress just generally New York crazy?

How many people had Finn met in his lifetime who were completely unlike himself and yet blended into society? Was Gabriel one of them too? It was hard not to question the people who'd had an impact on his life after a realization as stark as what he'd just witnessed.

Jasper was a magnificent tornado of intensity. He had real-life magical abilities, a seemingly naïve spirit, and porn-star sex appeal to boot. In just under an hour, he had managed to turn Finn's world on its head.

And Finn had the strangest feeling it was only just the beginning.

Inside his place he was sorely tempted to fix himself another drink. But it wouldn't do any good to go down that route. He had to keep his body in sound shape if he expected his mind to do the same.

Instead he went for a scorching hot shower and mulled over the day's events.

"Goddammit," he muttered to the tiles.

How was he supposed to go to work tomorrow sitting on this knowledge? Knowing that something entirely supernatural was living right across the street and there could be hundreds of others in this city and nobody had a clue?

When he stepped out of the shower, he was almost disappointed not to find another message from Jasper on the mirror. How stupid was that? This morning those messages were close to terrifying, and now he missed them?

Finn needed to sleep on what had happened to make sure it was real, and he prayed Jasper was smart enough to understand that making another appearance was a bad idea. As much as Finn felt a strange pull toward Jasper, it would only complicate things if he materialized now. And Finn didn't need any more complications in his life.

One devilishly charming and handsome young mage was definitely enough.

WORK WAS even more unproductive than Finn had anticipated.

He wasn't able to concentrate from the moment he woke to the moment he accepted everything Jasper had shown him. Turning a half-eaten Ding Dong into the most decadent cheesecake right in front of his eyes was no small feat, and there had been no room for sleight of hand.

Hopefully the board wouldn't check his internet search history, since Finn spent the better part of the day looking up fantasy creatures and famous conjurers. He was intrigued and what he found was both entertaining and educational—like how some people were convinced shapeshifters existed, like how some historical events didn't add up, and like how magical beings adorn themselves in jewelry because it grounds their spirits.

Gabriel took Finn's continued distraction as an opportunity to sway the staff. Throughout the day he planted seeds to promote TV chefs for the company, but Finn was too preoccupied to care.

As the day wore on, Finn found himself aching to get back to Jasper. He knew what he was going to do, so where was the sense playing hard to get? He didn't even bother to go home and shower after work. His entire being coursed with adrenaline, so he saved his legs and grabbed the elevator when he got to Jasper's.

This time, Finn was decidedly more confident knocking on the door of apartment 137B. He knew what to expect from the other side.

Jasper opened the door almost as soon as Finn's knuckles left the wood. There was a huge smile on his face, and he'd made an effort to dress up better than yesterday's sweats.

He was clad in a muscle-fit tee and linen short, and Finn's eyes went straight to his legs, which were surprisingly muscular and hairy. Jasper's grin got even bigger when Finn found his face again.

"Hey. Can I come in?"

"Certainly." Jasper held the door as Finn brushed past him and instantly noticed the difference in the apartment.

"This looks… um."

"Cleaner?" Jasper scoffed. "I know. It was pitiful before, and I'm sorry you had to see it."

"Don't be silly," said Finn. "You didn't have to do that."

Even if he was a little cautious, Jasper seemed to know how to behave around Finn—like an apprehensive cat. But then, he'd been watching Finn for more than a week straight. Finn was still unsure whether to feel creeped out or flattered by that part.

"So, what have you been doing today?" Finn asked, taking off his jacket and hanging it on a hook. "Shit, sorry. I forgot you can't leave."

"No worries," Jasper said, playing it cool as he moved to the kitchen. That seemed to be his favorite spot. Maybe it was because he could hide behind the counter and use it as some kind of physical barrier. "I've been trying to figure out how that came to be."

Jasper pointed to a stack of books off to the side, and Finn guessed that each brightly colored volume was easily a thousand pages long—not exactly light reading.

"Any luck?" Finn turned back to him.

"Zilch," Jasper replied. "I'm not exactly what you'd call an academic. Maybe you could help me look over them sometime?"

"Sure, whatever you want," Finn agreed and was surprised at how much he wanted to help.

Jasper breathed in deeply and let it out with a smile. "Thanks. Though I must stress that they can't leave this room."

"Oh, are they trapped as well?"

"No, I'm just asking you not to take them. They contain sensitive information, and I'm already in a shitload of trouble if anyone knows I've let you in on my secret."

"In trouble with whom?"

"The Magical Regulation Force."

"The who now?" Finn laughed. "Sounds like another Potter thing."

"I did mention them yesterday, but you were distracted, so it's fine. It's our version of police, and there are some very hefty implications for me telling you about my nature."

Finn wanted to fire another round of questions at Jasper, but he had to slow things down a bit after last time, get to know him a bit more before he probed deeper. Taking a seat on one of the barstools, Finn watched Jasper pour water from the kettle into a waiting mug.

Finn offered a questioning look.

"It was already boiled."

Huh. "So you *were* waiting for me?"

Jasper offered a knowing smile and bobbed his head to ask whether he wanted a cup. Finn shook his head and saw heat flush Jasper's cheeks. "I just… had a feeling you'd come back."

When Finn's eyebrows shot to the ceiling, Jasper merely winked.

"And you knew *when* I was coming back?" Finn wondered how it was Jasper had done so well to anticipate the change in his routine. "How much of my life do you know about?"

"Pretty much everything you do inside your home." The words were casual, juxtaposed with the weight of their meaning. "I haven't yet managed to follow you anywhere else."

Finn tried to feel better about that, but it didn't work. His home was his private sanctuary where he could unwind and be totally alone. Apparently that wasn't the case any longer. Jesus… had this guy seen him jerking off under the couch blanket? Or seen the men he'd try to hook up with only to end up ducking out last minute? Did Jasper think him a timewasting catfish? Would he now have to explain his intimacy issues when he didn't even understand them himself?

Finn's world was closing in on him again, and Jasper was quick to notice.

"For what it's worth, I'm not sorry."

Oh. That was bold.

"Well," Finn started, "don't you think it was a bit invasive?"

"Oh yeah, I guess," Jasper said, crinkling his eyes in a lopsided smile. "Well, I am sorry about that bit! But I was—excuse me, I *am*—in need of help. And I finally got to meet you." He paused to sip his drink and made sure to make a show of licking the moisture from his lips. "I know things are crazy right now, but it'll be worth it in the end."

"Will it, indeed?" Finn tried to tap into his flirting charisma, but he'd never been good at the damned thing. He'd given up on the idea of dating ages ago when all the fabricated drama that came with them messed with his work life. Things seemed different here, and Finn would've given him a double thumbs up if it didn't feel so '80s. "What makes you so sure?"

"I'm here, you're here," said Jasper. "Anything could happen."

"WOULD YOU like a bite?" Jasper asked.

Finn had been admiring the various paintings dotted around the room for the last five or so minutes, and he was curious to see what Jasper kept under that tarp. If memory served, he'd been hasty to cover it up yesterday. Though Finn respected the unspoken code of privacy, he was still curious, especially given that half of the pictures were of attractive nude men, and Jasper had some serious talent with phallic interpretations.

"I'm fine, thanks," Finn said when he figured out that Jasper was referring to food, not anything lewd. Jasper seemed a little hurt at the rejection, so Finn switched tactics when he remembered what he could do. "On second thought… I could eat."

Jasper's ability had knocked his socks off the first time, and now that he was in the mage's apartment for a second time, Finn was comfortable enough to be open with his reaction. And who knows… perhaps it was linked with his bizarre entrapment?

"What would you like, then?"

That was a broad question. "I suppose it depends on the limits of your skill."

"Imagine there are none." Jasper winked. Flirting seemed to come easy for him, and Finn made a conscious effort to at least match it if he couldn't beat it. "I only have to read a recipe once to master the creation of it. I was a chef back in my hometown, so believe me when I tell you I've read my fair share."

"Oh? Where are you from originally?"

"Providence, Rhode Island." There was an automatic grin on Jasper's face that probably wasn't meant for Finn. It was clear the place held good memories, which wasn't too surprising, given that he was indefinitely trapped here. "I had such dreams coming to the Big Apple."

"I take it these are part of that?" Finn jerked his head toward the canvases. "They're by far the most creative thing I've seen all year… and I like to think I know a thing or two about art."

"I'll say," Jasper whispered. He probably got that Finn was the kind of guy who didn't hand out compliments needlessly. "My plan was to go showcase some of the… uh… more family-friendly ones in some exhibitions. But as a result of this predicament, I've missed out on three of the most reputable summer spots. Suffice to say I'm having second thoughts about moving here."

Finn offered a weak smile. "Whatever's going on here might've also happened back there. Unless someone in the city has placed a curse on you or something?"

"Ha-ha." Jasper pushed at Finn's knee and nearly made his leg fall off of its perch on the other one. When Jasper drew his hand away, Finn wanted more contact. There was heat crackling around the air, but it was too soon to even think about acting on it. "I did wonder if it was the work of an ex or maybe my parents… though it seems unlikely. The Magical Regulation Force would know if such a spell were cast, and it would've been resolved before now if that were the case."

Interesting. That was a topic worth exploring later. "Don't give up," Finn offered. "Maybe you'll be able to make that show after all."

"Pfft," Jasper whistled through his teeth. "Don't joke about that. I'm almost at my breaking point here. So, what's on the menu for us tonight?"

Finn choked on air, then realized it wasn't yet another flawlessly interjected innuendo. He had genuinely forgotten that Jasper was about to show his talent again. It seemed Jasper was so charismatic that Finn had been all-too distracted from his magical food abilities. That probably spoke volumes.

"How about coq au vin?" Finn tried. Jasper might not have cooked that before, and he was keen to test boundaries. "With some salted focaccia and crispy duchess potatoes?"

"Coming right up," Jasper agreed without missing a beat, and Finn watched his tight little ass sashay to the kitchen. "Seems you've got good taste, Muscles."

"*Muscles*?" croaked Finn as he followed. "Oh, so that's all I am to you? Just a big hunk of man meat?" Finn kept the smirk on his face as Jasper whipped around. "I'm kidding, obviously. Who wouldn't want to worship these guns?" When Finn pulled a swan pose and made the cotton of his shirt bulge as he flexed his biceps, he enjoyed the glazed-over look on Jasper's face a little too much. "Sorry, I'm not that vain, I promise. Anyway, just how is it you're able to live here, by the way? Are you running some kind of ridiculously impractical drug den to pay rent?"

Jasper stopped arranging casserole dishes and base ingredients long enough to shoot a sharp glance.

"Sorry," Finn offered. "My turn being intrusive. Don't answer that."

Jasper shrugged and set back to work. "Sometimes being direct is best. I'm out of practice with social cues. Suspicious of everyone, you know?"

"Could've fooled me. You're doing better than I am, and I talk to dozens of people every day."

"Interesting," Jasper mused. Finn wasn't sure whether Jasper was referring to him or the food laid out in front of him. Most of the items looked a bit past their use-by date, and though it made him slightly queasy, Finn wasn't about to interrupt a ritual he knew nothing about. "My friends," Jasper continued, "the ones you saw yesterday? They're currently subsidizing my rent. I worked in a bakery when I first got here, but I lost the job when I became… otherwise engaged."

"Damn. That's real nice of them, though. Some good friends you got there."

"They really are." When Jasper finally deemed himself finished, he placed his hands a few inches above the dishes and closed his eyes. "Maybe you could meet them soon. Like, properly."

"Maybe," said Finn. "But not too soon, eh?"

That was Finn's way of saying he was happy with just Jasper's company for now. Jasper cracked open an eye and grinned to show he understood.

There was a tinge of blue beneath Jasper's hands, and a gurgling sound echoed around the room as the ingredients transformed themselves from grimy mush to a Michelin-star-level meal. It was a wonderous thing to behold, something Finn knew he would never tire of seeing, and it wasn't long before Jasper opened his eyes again and they both stared at an array of food fit for a king's banquet. Any trace of rot had been eradicated as though it were never there.

"Holy shit."

And that was before the beautiful medley of aromas hit him. He could already taste how heavenly it was as Jasper put a spoon in the dish and pushed it down the counter.

"That's art, if ever I saw it."

"Dive on in," Jasper said, that ever-present charm lingering around him as naturally as the bewitching scent of food. "Grab it while it's hot."

"You don't need to tell me twice," Finn said, feeling like a kid again as he spooned promised decadence onto his plate.

CHAPTER SIX

FINN WAS a delightful guest—totally the opposite of the man Jasper had first pigeonholed him as.

It was nice to spend quality time with someone other than Mikasa and Elijah, with their fleeting visits. Though he appreciated their company, they never stayed long. He promised himself the next time they came over, he'd make them stay for dinner.

They didn't chat much during the meal, mostly because Finn kept making cute sounds of appreciation and digging back in for more. He wasn't doing it just to be kind either, as when Jasper was full to bursting, Finn asked if he could polish off his plate.

"Go for it," Jasper said. "I saw that look from before, by the way. When you looked at the rotting food? Because my gift can reverse the state back to peak quality, I get Mikasa and Elijah to collect cast-offs from cafés and bistros for next to nothing. To be honest, I'm glad I don't have to be the one to endure any weird looks."

"Wow," Finn mused. "So you're, like, recycling the city's produce? That's genius."

Jasper smiled by way of thanks. "Care for some of the good stuff? I never used to like whiskey until a few weeks ago. Funny what the brain gets used to when you're stuck staring at the same four walls."

Nodding in confirmation, Finn chewed quickly to sneak in another question while Jasper popped the cork.

"Does your ability work on drinks as well?" There was a look of pure wonder in Finn's eyes. Since nobody had ever taken half as much interest with Jasper's gift as Finn had, he was almost reluctant to give the answer.

"Unfortunately, no." Jasper made sure to fill up the tumbler at least three-quarters of the way, so he wouldn't have to keep getting up when they inevitably transitioned over to the couch. "Not sure why. Everyone has a unique gift in some way. No two mage-born have the exact same ability."

"Is that so?"

"Yeah. We categorize ourselves by comparable skills, though they're never exactly the same. I'm a transmuter, like I said before, but I can't do anything fancy *and* practical. No water to wine or lead to gold or anything *actually* useful." He handed Finn the drink and tucked his feet under himself. "There's a dusty old tome locked away in the main spire of the high library where every mage's abilities are kept on record. That way we can sort of police it if necessary. Nothing bad ever happens, though."

"Damn." Finn absently eyed the paintings. "The mind really boggles at what people can do. Couldn't someone have the power to see into the future and pick the winning lottery numbers?"

"Nope. I mean, someone *could* have such a power of foresight, but our magisters would know if a gift gets extremely abused."

"How?"

"When something *big* happens that goes against the rules, it creates an energy shift. Some high-up guys have a sort of echolocation for other people's powers. Kind of like thought police but less dramatic. So when something bad happens, the detectors can pinpoint them."

"Detectors?" Finn's brow wrinkled. "Like detectives?"

"Yep. It's a handsomely paid job."

"I'll bet. Could other people use their powers for money? Are there separate prisons for you guys?"

"Of course there are." Jasper laughed through his nose. "Some people are simply batshit through and through, Finn. Powers or not."

Finn nodded his head. "If that isn't the truth. I wonder what ability I'd have if I were mage-born."

"Something to do with your eyes, I'll bet. Like Mikasa's telekinesis—it wouldn't work if she were blind. She's got lovely eyes, but yours…? Yours are way better." He leaned in a little closer, hoping it wasn't too bold. "It's like someone shattered the moon and left a trail of stardust in your irises."

"Wow," Finn breathed. "Most people say I've got cold, calculating eyes. Thanks for that."

Jasper hoped the sentiment would be reciprocated, and he tried not to beat himself up when it wasn't.

"I feel bad for the poor bastard who has the gift to alter liquids. This one's bad enough."

Finn wiped the corners of his mouth with a napkin. "You think *this*… is bad?" He'd spread out his hands to indicate the food Jasper had produced.

"Well, yeah." Jasper shrugged, handing him the glass and pouring wine for himself. "You should see what others can do. My family's abilities alone are enough to overthrow the government if they wanted."

Finn arched an eyebrow. "You could probably start revolutions of your own with food like this."

Jasper let out a carefree giggle, happy the tension was slipping away. He was having the most fun he'd had in months, and it was curious how laughter seemed to mend the soul. With Finn sitting across from him, it already felt like years worth of repressed damage lifting.

"Shall we?" Jasper asked, motioning to the couch. "There isn't much to do around here, what with the lack of television."

"I'm sure you could find ways to entertain me," Finn said, sipping his drink.

To stop himself from jumping Finn's bones right there, Jasper swiped a book from the stack.

"This is my latest read," Jasper informed, passing it over when they got to the couch. Since he was first to sit down, Jasper deliberately left some space, and he was glad Finn chose to sit next to him.

"Christ," Finn commented. "This thing weighs a ton."

Jasper stared at the point where their knees met, trying to keep innuendos at bay. "There's another bookcase in my bedroom filled to the brim with books just like that. Most of them were gifts from old friends I've left behind, but I brought them here to New York by way of remembering them. I've only managed to get through about half."

"*Plana Aereum*?" Finn tested, flipping over to skim the blurb.

"It's Latin. Super dramatic, I know."

"Wow," Finn said after flipping it open to the page Jasper had dogeared. "I might need a magnifying glass for this. Why would they make the text this small?"

"You get used to it after a while," Jasper assured. "Hard to believe there's four more volumes after this one, though."

Finn took a long sip of his drink, then reached over to place it on the coffee table, took the book in both hands, and stroked the pages. Maybe this was a mistake. Not long ago, Jasper was jealous of pigeons. Now he was envious of a book?

Whatever next?

"If you align yourself properly, you can achieve a perfect state of balance, therein allowing you to transverse throughout the plane." Finn looked up for affirmation, and Jasper gave it to him in the form of a nod. "Is this how you managed to project yourself?"

"Sure is."

"And you're only halfway through the first of five books?"

"Seems that way." Jasper sipped his wine, edged himself a little bit closer to Finn, and prayed he didn't immediately notice.

"Imagine what else you could do…," Finn dreamed. "The mind baffles. Like, could you do sexual stuff in the astral plane?"

Eyes popping out of his skull, Jasper almost spat wine over Finn and the book. Finn was shrewd and fast enough to place it on the table, out of the danger zone, and pick up his own drink.

"Being bold again. Sorry." Finn grinned. Jasper knew his latest apology was just lip service… and he was fine with that. "My hand went straight through you when I touched you that first time you appeared. Yet you were able to interact with my mirror before then. Am I to assume it's a one-way thing?"

"Honestly," Jasper started, "I have no idea. But I'm more than willing to find out."

They'd had a bit to drink, so the flirting ramped up. Jasper wasn't ashamed at all. It was rewarding to finally have someone walk into his life. Finn got him. Even after spending so little physical time with him, Jasper knew it. And Finn had to know it too.

The moment was almost broken when Finn stole a glance at the watch on his wrist. In spite of the time, his voice took on a suggestive tone. "It's getting pretty late."

"Yeah," Jasper agreed. Getting lost in Finn's eyes, the last thing Jasper wanted was for him to leave. It was probably too soon to jump into bed with him. There were instant attractions, and then there were burnout relationships. The latter would suck.

"Maybe you could stay?" Jasper couldn't help himself.

Finn pulled back. It was only by a little, but it felt like miles.

"I only live across the road," Finn said. A very astute observation. Again, it sounded like he was open to suggestion.

"But it's such a long, hard walk," Jasper snarked. "I wouldn't want you to venture out in the darkness alone. Not after a big glass of whiskey."

Finn's body language was hinting that Jasper might get his way, but he knew the man's moral compass was trembling.

"You can take my bed," Jasper suggested. "Even though it's probably not a tenth as nice as what you're used to. I'll take the couch."

Finn sighed through his nose, gaze flitting back and forth to Jasper's, no doubt desperate to come up with a reason why he shouldn't.

"All right," Finn agreed. "But first, let me test something."

Jasper was about to ask what the hell he was going on about when Finn closed what little gap was left between them and planted his mouth on Jasper's.

Lit up with an array of blinding color, every nerve ending in Jasper's body was set ablaze as Finn explored his mouth. Finn's rough day-old stubble scratched him, and he could taste the bitterness from the liquor. There were hints of minty sweetness there too, and Jasper itched for more. When Finn raked a hand through Jasper's hair and pulled him down to make their bodies meet, the drink fell from his hands. Fuck it. The carpet was ruined anyway.

Jasper would set the damn thing on fire to satisfy his need.

Finn sighed and pressed his weight onto Jasper so together they sank farther into the couch. Jasper could feel himself get hard through his shorts, and when he arched his hips, rocking them for Finn to rub up against, there was no denying Finn's purpose. He wanted more contact, more intimacy. Skin on skin. Flesh against flesh.

Jasper was a lust-craved fangirl after prom, and they moaned into each other's mouths as Finn cupped Jasper's chin and tickled the nape of his neck.

"You're so fucking hot," Finn whispered, sending a barrage of quivers up to Jasper's scalp. "I can't get enough of you."

Finn paired the hot breathy whispers with a smattering of cool kisses down Jasper's neck. His skin was hypersensitive, teetering on the edge of overwhelming. It was utter madness—mad that he could feel such joy from such simple acts and mad that he wasn't combusting right then and there.

Through his pants Jasper gripped Finn's rock-solid length and began to caress it roughly. He was frantic at that point, and he wanted to please Finn in every sense of the word—make him realize just how much he deserved a damn good servicing. Just as things were starting to get interesting, Finn pulled them both upright in one forceful swoop, then made time stand still as he grazed his bottom lip with his teeth.

Finn studied Jasper, and there was something primal in his eyes, as though all it would take was one more naughty glance for him to flip off caution and plow Finn right there on the couch... but he was too hesitant. This wasn't their time to conquer the world, and Jasper knew it took a metric fuck ton of restraint for Finn to peck Jasper one more time before he got up to retreat to the bedroom.

Melting on the inside, Jasper wanted to call out to Finn, to beg for him to come back and finish the job. His dick was harder than a diamond and ready for a wild night of endless pleasure, but even through the semidrunken haze of wine, Jasper knew some things were worth waiting for.

He just prayed that day came sooner rather than later.

CHAPTER SEVEN

FINN'S HEART almost gave out when he woke and didn't instantly recognize his surroundings. Then he remembered why the bed underneath him was considerably smaller and considerably lumpier, and why he was surrounded by bookcases and a heap of unfinished paintings.

He was in Jasper's bed. And he had kissed him last night. It hadn't just been a small kiss either. It had been intense, passionate, with a great deal of dry humping.

Why, oh why, had he done that? Had the mage compelled him beyond his human nature? Finn didn't think so. Jasper's remarkably Cheyenne Jackson–esque features paired with his straight-to-the-point approach easily made him the sexiest man Finn had ever met, and as he climbed out of bed and saw the morning sun crest over the city's lowest skyscrapers, Finn didn't feel an ounce of remorse about his actions.

When his gaze drifted up to his place, an enormous grin threatened to split his face in half.

Last night he'd had more fun in Jasper's apartment than he'd had in weeks at his own. They were onto a good thing, he and Jasper. Stretching out his limbs, Finn wondered how Jasper thought about it—the kiss, specifically. Had Finn forced himself on him? He'd only had two whiskeys, and Jasper had supplied them with obvious intent.

Finn wasn't to blame for getting carried away.

Since he didn't have the luxury of an en suite to preen himself, he used the full-length mirror. He looked passable in a rough-and-ready kind of way. Hardly the norm… but then, things weren't exactly normal lately.

"Morning." Jasper was on the couch, golden hair splayed wildly over the fabric, book in hand with the dawn light filtering past his jaw.

"Hi," Finn replied, trying and failing to act casual. He scratched the back of his head and wished it were appropriate to jump in his lap and cuddle up with him. "Thanks for letting me have the bed."

"Pfft," Jasper huffed and waved a hand. "You're too polite. That busted old thing could never compare to your four-poster."

Finn's automatic smile wavered when he remembered Jasper had been snooping around his place for the past week without his knowledge. They would have to get into the ethics of that later on.

"Would you like some breakfast?" Sticking a bookmark in his paperback, Jasper made to get up, but Finn held up his hand.

"No, thanks. I've gotta get to work." There was clear disappointment on Jasper's face. Finn was disappointed too. After last night's meal, he couldn't even imagine what Jasper could magic up for breakfast. "Sorry. Maybe next time?"

That seemed to perk Jasper up. It also put Finn in better spirits to verbalize the possibility of a next time.

Jasper tossed the book on the coffee table and let it become another piece of debris in the mountainous Jenga tower. Then he got to his feet.

Damn. Finn didn't think anyone could look desirable in plaid pajamas, but the ensemble fit Jasper's body like a glove and didn't leave much to the imagination.

Mentally pinching himself, Finn focused on Jasper's face.

"Will you come back tonight?" Jasper asked. "You can't imagine how dull it is to sit around here on my ass day after day. It's amazing I haven't gained two hundred pounds from my lack of exercise. Some company would be nice, because Mikasa and Elijah only visit twice a week."

Finn wrinkled his nose, unsure whether to make the promise. He needed some breathing room, if only to solidify his feelings or to work out what they actually were.

"I'll see if I can make it," he said noncommittally. "Things are a bit crazy at work right now. I've got a lot on my plate."

"It's cool." With eyes low, Jasper said, "I get it."

Now things were awkward. Finn wanted to turn and leave, but he didn't want to part on a sour note. Though he'd kissed Jasper last night, he didn't feel like he could just waltz up and do it again.

Maybe he could settle with a hug.

"I'd be happy to see you again," Finn said as he walked up, arms open. Jasper tilted his head, a brief look of *really?* written on his face. But he returned the hug, and Finn pulled him tight to his body, taking in faint notes of apricot and bergamot.

But Finn didn't anticipate the true awkwardness of a hug, and when they let each other go, there was that inevitable moment of to kiss or not to kiss.

Jasper's stormy blue eyes flitted back and forth with Finn's, and the seconds felt like minutes. Unable to stand the wait any longer, Finn kissed him on the cheek.

Jasper let out a soft chuckle, and it resonated in Finn's bones.

"Have a good day, Muscles."

As Finn walked out, he scratched the back of his neck again. This time it was simply to hide the scorching heat flushing in his skin.

BECAUSE HE had to pop back home and make himself presentable for the office, Finn ran the risk of being late again.

This time as he scrambled about his apartment, he was jittery from excitement rather than unease. Though his life was still organized chaos, Jasper was doing a good job of brightening it. Plus, he'd gotten to the bottom of the mystery that had been bugging him, and he was happy with the result.

When Finn got out of the Uber and up to the office, his mood nosedived the instant he saw Gabriel's face.

"Look, Finn," he said, wasting no time with preamble as they walked. "Your dad's breathing down my neck to get this shit sorted out. He backs up your ideas, believe it or not, so you should probably take advantage of that while you can."

Finn stopped in his tracks, positive he hadn't heard correctly. When did Gabriel ever dish out personal advice that wasn't to benefit himself? "Are you feeling all right?"

"Fine," said Gabriel, impatience written all over his face. "I'm just over this impasse. It would help everyone around us if we worked together."

"Right," said Finn. "Are you sure someone didn't spike your coffee?"

"Ha-ha," Gabriel sneered. "We need to stop butting heads and come up with something fast. Like, now."

"What do you propose?"

"A mixer," Gabriel said, hand on Finn's door. "Maybe if we can put together a swanky event, it'll attract all the high rollers. The sponsors always get the best deals, and we'll snap up some new talent in no time."

"Sounds good," Finn said, surprised with himself for agreeing so quickly. "Let's get started."

THE NIGHT-AND-DAY change in Gabriel's mood was more than welcome. It was the first day in a solid year where he wasn't acting like a thorn in Finn's side, and the difference in his own mood was marked because of it.

They'd been shut inside Finn's office for the better part of two hours and had just finalized the profit margins for what was going to be an expensive night—expensive, but worth it.

"Who would've thought we could actually work together?" Finn joked, marveling at the final form of the spreadsheet they had created.

"I know, right?" Gabriel glanced up from his fountain pen, then went back to scribbling some different figures. "Amazing what can happen when you don't stare at my ass all day."

Finn bit back a retort he would've had no qualms about earlier that week. Working as a team, they had made better progress in half a day than a full month at each other's throats.

As he closed Excel and responded to some internal queries, Finn wondered if his father would bother to get on a plane to attend the event. Always dressed in the latest Gucci, Finn's dad relished any chance to show off his wealth, and since he would ultimately be paying for the event, there was no doubt he'd be waiting on the sidelines to pull the puppet strings.

"Where are those notes on healthy living?" Gabriel held his hand out.

"Right here." Finn scoured a stack of documents, passed the notes across, and was rewarded with a small smile. "Whoa, take it down a notch, dude. Anyone would think you might actually respect me as a person."

Gabriel snorted. "Let's just get meeting number 264 over with, shall we?"

MADISON WAS too busy juggling new content to attend the meeting, and Shelly wasn't comfortable sitting in on it because she couldn't stand Gabriel's leering eyes. Which meant only Finn and Gabriel were in the conference room waiting in front of a blank screen, and Finn was drumming his pen on his notepad to fill the empty silence.

"Will you stop that?" Scowling, Gabriel wiped his hands on his pants. "Avery sure likes to keep us waiting, doesn't he?"

"Yep. I think he does it to remind us of the power he has. All it does is make him seem unprofessional."

"Is that so?" came a thunderous simulated voice. Finn had been too busy daydreaming to notice his father's likeness flicker onto the screen, and by the grim set of his face, he wasn't impressed. "If you must know," he continued, "I just lost a sale on a five-bed condo in Miami. So, I truly hope the pair of you have something good for me."

"We've got a mixer prepared," said Gabriel, sifting through his notes. "Venue's booked, props are ordered, and everything's paid for. Just need to invite some guests."

"Make sure they're high-profile," Avery ordered. "There's no sense draining my bank account if we don't have some rich suckers to fill it right back up. Also, make sure you push the brand at every chance you get. I want *Zest* on everyone's brain and lips before they leave. I want the men thinking about it when they go to the gym and the ladies talking about it between their lunch dates."

Finn was tired of the outdated view, and he was getting pretty sick of being told things he already knew. "Won't you be attending, yourself?"

"Sadly not." The little grin on Avery's face said he was anything but sad. "I've got three more viewings tomorrow, a meeting with the bank the day after that, and Jennif…. Mrs. Anderson… tells me there's a hot up-and-coming deal on bulk smartwatches from the Korean exchange. Could be onto a winner."

As Gabriel made some notes—probably to avoid eye contact—Finn pinched his nose. The fact that Finn's mom was now apparently clued up on stock exchanges wasn't necessarily a surprise. She would do just about anything to keep her purse brimming with cash. No, what bothered Finn was that he'd genuinely thought his dad would oversee the mixer, and deep down, it stung that he had distanced himself to the point that he was now so far removed from the company that he probably wouldn't care if they peddled drugs if it meant scoring a profit.

"How is it you always manage to take the high ground?" Finn asked. Silence followed, and Finn could feel the disbelief radiating from Avery's digital waves. Instead of caving and apologizing, he took a sip of water. "I mean, it's pretty clear you don't have any interest in what we're doing here. We're supposed to be championing locally grown produce and incentivizing sustainable practices. When was the last time you ate anything that wasn't corn-fed?"

"Excuse me for thinking two of my finest lemmings could take care of it. That *is* what I pay you for, isn't it?" The question sounded rhetorical, but Avery wanted an answer. "Well?" His raised voice crackled through the speakers. "Can you or can you not handle it?"

Finn was about to say something, but Gabriel butted in. "We can, sir. With respect, Finn doesn't know what he's talking about. He's too stuck on saving the planet from things like global warming.

Little does he know the damage has already been done, and it's people like you and me, sir, who learn how to profit from it."

In a flash, Mr. Nice Guy was gone. The happy-go-lucky Gabriel from before was nowhere to be seen as he turned on Finn, and Avery was quite clearly pleased to see it.

"Interesting," said Avery. "I can't say I appreciate your tone, but this is the kind of ruthless attitude we need to employ if we're goi–"

The feed jittered, sending a grainy, distorted version of his dad's face as he garbled out the rest of the sentence in incoherent stutters. When the screen went blue and showed a silvery dial attempting to reconnect, Finn whirled to the side to face Gabriel.

"What the fuck are you doing, man? We were cool not even an hour ago!"

Gabriel shrugged. "Just doing my job, Finny. Not my fault if your name gets tarnished in the process."

"Suck-up," Finn spat. "You'd probably hop on his dick if it meant getting that promotion."

"Yeah, well, so what if I did?" Gabriel sniggered. "What are you gonna do about it? You wouldn't dare walk out on two meetings in a week. You're too busy living off daddy's money to do anything that would jeopardize your lifestyle."

"Yeah?" Finn said, getting to his feet. "Just fucking watch me."

Finn wasn't too pleased with himself as he stormed out of the room, especially as the screen had just reconnected. He'd fallen for Gabriel's bait, and that bastard was probably filling Avery's head with some twisted bullshit. But Finn let him get on with it. He never normally let words hurt him, but it was the disrespectful undertones from the callous men that really seemed to burn.

Though it was two hours before his day was supposed to end, he couldn't stand a minute longer in that building. He took some of the notes from his desk, caught the subway home, and was too pressed to go for his postwork coffee. He was also too pissed off to even think about visiting Jasper.

Finn recognized the signs of a volatile mood and knew it wouldn't do any good—he might end up lashing out at Jasper when he in no way deserved it.

Instead of thinking about blossoming relationships or anything work-related, Finn gave in to a guilty pleasure and sank himself into the couch in front of the television. He hoped to lose a few brain cells watching a box set of senseless sitcoms.

CHAPTER EIGHT

JASPER'S DAY consisted of painting, reading—both educational and fictional—using his gift to cook, some light cleaning, and thinking about Finn. He'd given up on the cleaning pretty quickly and was spending what little remained of the daylight watching the street below.

From his vantage point, there were many brash conversations to overhear and so many times he could be disappointed that he couldn't join them. It was a grim fascination that pulled Jasper in to watch and listen every day. It had become his routine, and he could no more help himself than a dog could help burying a bone.

The sun was just beginning to dip below the skyscrapers when Jasper's attention was caught by a man in a suit. Checking his clock in the kitchen, it was too soon for the nine-to-fivers to clock off. When he turned back and pressed his nose up against the window to get a better look, Jasper's mouth fell open when he realized the businessman was Finn.

He was coming home early. Tingles fizzed in the pit of Jasper's stomach, and he was just about to get up and put the kettle on when Finn didn't cross the road to come to him. Instead, he carried on to his building and dashed into the revolving doors with a disconcerted look on his face.

Jasper's brow furrowed, but instead of getting ahead of himself, his gaze went skyward and he waited for Finn to come into his apartment. Maybe he was just getting changed or fetching a gift for Jasper. There must be a good reason why he'd dipped out of work early.

When Finn threw his briefcase across the floor, switched on the television, and jumped onto the couch, Jasper's heart sank. He couldn't pretend he wasn't hurt as it was pretty clear Finn had settled himself in for the long haul. He might as well have tucked himself up with a blanket and Ben & Jerry's.

Getting up off the window ledge, Jasper made himself a coffee and tried to settle his thoughts with the roasted aroma.

When he left that morning, Finn had all but promised to come around later on. Jasper's first thought was to project himself into his place and get answers to his questions. But he was also a shrewd enough adult to realize that was a stupid idea. Finn obviously had his reasons why he wasn't following through on his promise, but instead of jumping to erratic conclusions, thinking they were done before they had any chance to gain momentum, Jasper restrained himself.

Maybe work really was getting on top of Finn. Jasper wanted to find ways to help, but he couldn't recall Finn ever telling him what his job role actually was.

Well, shit. Sitting on the ledge with coffee in hand, Jasper went back to people watching. He tried very hard not to keep tabs on Finn, but every so often, something would catch his peripheral vision, and he would find his eyes lifting with a mind of their own.

CHAPTER NINE

WHEN FINN woke up, he sincerely hoped yesterday was just a dream. Working alongside Gabriel for years, he'd come to expect snide remarks and even cutting comments that almost always stretched the truth. But genuine contempt from his own dad? That was something else.

He was pushy, he was money-obsessed, and he was certainly on his way to being ruthless. Fine. But had he entirely forgotten that Finn was his son? What could that mean for their future?

Yanking himself out of bed, Finn dragged his feet to the shower and went through his usual motions. He was back to normal until it came to climbing on the elliptical for a hard workout. Just minutes after he started it up and got into a decent rhythm, his gaze automatically lowered from the skyline and trailed down to Jasper's apartment.

Sure enough, a miniature version of the mage was at his window, crimson-tipped paintbrush stroking the face of a canvas with his hair tied up in a tight little bun that was actually neat and tidy for once.

That's when everything fell into place and Finn felt like he was seeing color for the first time. How could he have been so damn blind?

"Holy shit." Pressing the Emergency Stop button, he stood in place, panting as he stared at the intent look on Jasper's face.

Finn had completed a degree in business and a master's in management, and yet he couldn't see what was right in front of his face. How had he not seen it before? Jasper was the key to everything— happiness, success, prosperity, both mentally and physically. Everything would work out better than a charming little fairy tale if

Finn could just trust himself and the possibility of a relationship, and not just in the romantic sense.

Screw the mixer. Screw Gabriel. Screw Avery. In fact, screw the whole job itself if it really came down to it. A million thoughts raced through Finn's mind as he grabbed yesterday's notes and bolted down the stairs. All he could think about was Jasper and all the potential they had between them.

"Shit!" Once again, Finn had lost track of time, and he was surprised to find his morning Uber parked up outside, waiting with engine idling.

"Hey, listen," said Finn, leaning down to the man's open window. "Could you do me a huge favor? Would you drive back to my work and hand these notes in to the front desk? Tell the receptionist they're for Gabriel Fernandez."

"You kidding?" was the gruff response. "I got places to be, bud. I'm on a tight schedule. You know, to actually drive people around?"

"Here." Finn reached into his pocket and handed over a hundred-dollar bill. He could have promised to do it electronically via the app's tipping service, but the situation called for immediate gratification. "Consider it a bonus. For excellent service."

The driver's cranky scowl transformed before Finn's eyes, and he grabbed the money and the keynotes without so much as a thank-you and drove off. Finn panicked for all of five seconds when he realized the guy might just take the cash and run. But he had the driver's profile on his cell, and if the job wasn't completed, he'd be sure to give a scathing review.

By the time he raced across the street and ran up to Jasper's apartment because someone was using the elevator, Finn was out of breath. When he got to the door, he beat on it with his fists.

"Finn?" Jasper opened the door, plainly surprised to see him. "Aren't you supposed to be at wo—"

"You're the answer," Finn interrupted, barging past. "You're my answer."

"Eh?" When Jasper closed the door and turned around, he wiped his paint-covered hands on his apron. "You're not making sense."

"All along I've been stressing over this stuff… and the key was right here. I was just too stupid to see it before… and now I know."

"Just take a breath and slow down, Finn. Would you like a drink?"

He shook his head vigorously, grinning from ear to ear. "I'm just so excited. Everything could work out now."

"Why, though?" Jasper untied his apron, sat on the couch, and patted a spot next to him. "Come sit and talk to me."

Finn did as he was asked and then put a hand on Jasper's knee and gripped tight. "You can save my business. Or at least, we can create a new one."

"We can?" Jasper wore the perfect expression of puzzlement. "And how are we going to do that?"

"With your talents, of course." Finn threw his own hands up in the air. "You make the best food in the world out of thin air. Imagine what you could do if you combined it with the thing you love."

The confusion was still evident. "And what's that?"

"Your artwork, silly. If you can marry your talent as a painter with your other abilities, we'd be the talk of New York. Maybe even the world…."

Jasper shook his head, smiling. "I'm still a bit lost. Maybe you could explain to me what it is you actually do for a living?"

"Oh, right," Finn snorted. He was acting crazy dumb lately, and he pegged it on Jasper's wily looks and disarming nature. "I work for a food company that used to print magazines, but now it's an app… and you have a magical ability that lets you transform food. I'm so dumb for not considering this before."

"Interesting." Jasper arched an eyebrow. "I had you down as an accountant or real estate agent with those captivating eyes and that soothing aura."

"Huh. My father would probably prefer that, because he just doesn't *get* what I'm trying to do," Finn moaned. "When I moved here and got my first set of subscribers to the magazine, it gave highlights to our work and showcased the people growing our produce, and it was so promising. I enjoyed writing the code for the online version as much as I liked reading the magazine, because local people were being recognized for the work they were doing."

Jasper hummed. "And they aren't getting that same recognition with the app?"

"Nope," Finn sighed. "There's this one celeb chef—Steven. He got his own show on Fox recently, so it was a 'must have' for him to have a section on the app where people can interact with his avatar after they sit through three ads. I don't want to sell out the moment we start seeing dollar signs. I don't want to spend my days forever optimizing performance and pushing user engagement for the *right* kind of advertisement revenue. I want to see people's creativity succeed. This company was built on championing the little guys, and I'll be damned if I have to keep pandering to this era where all we do is incessantly appease social media."

"Hey, I get it." Jasper held his hands up in surrender, apparently not about to pick a fight with something Finn cared for so strongly. "I know more than anyone how soul-crushing it is to not get the recognition you deserve as an artist. There are very few people with your kind of outlook. It's uplifting."

"Thanks," Finn said. His grin got wider at the unexpected compliment, and he lost track of the conversation as he and Jasper continued to examine each other's faces. "So. What do you think about working together on something? It'll be, like, *the* easiest thing to do. As long as you have the ingredients in front of you, you can transform them into edible pieces of art with that amazing, complex brain of yours."

Shrugging, Jasper figured it wasn't entirely impossible for that to work. "How would it pan out in the business sense? I mean, will we share the profits fifty-fifty? Or is that too greedy? I don't even know how to do my own taxes."

"Cute," Finn commented. "I don't see why we wouldn't split profits down the middle. We're equals in every sense of the word. You make the art, and I'll find us venues and get the sponsors. Just got to make sure everything is locally grown and sourced, and from there, all we need is some kind of kick-start to get some initial recognition. With enough interest, it'll soon snowball."

"Sounds pretty promising," said Jasper.

"We don't have to come up with all of the specifics right now. But I can message Gabriel and tell him I'll be in later if you want to chat about it."

Jasper stood up and paced over to the window with his back to Finn. "I think you're a little too excited. It's adorable," he muttered and turned back around. "But you seem to have forgotten the predicament I'm in."

"Oh?" Still rippling with adrenaline, Finn got up from the couch and crossed over Jasper. "Oh yeah. Sorry, I guess I did. You have to admit, it is an unusual one."

Jasper shrugged.

"There's nothing stopping us from doing it here, though." Finn allowed himself to get carried away again with all the possibilities. "I can bring you all the stuff, you can do your magic, and we'll be rich as pigs before fall hits."

"Excuse me?" Jasper frowned. "So, when you go out to live your normal, everyday life, I'll just stay in here, cramped up like the cliché of a pathetic artist?"

When he realized the day-to-day effect of what he was suggesting, Finn extended a hand for comfort. Thankfully Jasper's anger was short-lived, but Finn kicked himself.

He felt like an ass for not being more sensitive and helpful. When he saw the potential in something incredible for them to do together— regardless that it would undoubtedly help him as a businessman—he was desperate to find any excuse to spend more time with Jasper.

Slowly, Finn cupped Jasper's chin and turned his face up to meet his gaze.

"I guess we'll just have to work on breaking you out."

Chapter Ten

Jasper gazed at Finn's face and searched for hints of mockery. But there were none. He really meant what he said.

There was nothing but determination in Finn's continued stare, and Jasper still had a hard time believing Finn was real, that he'd gotten so lucky to have a man as outrageously sexy and level-headed want to help. Whether he actually *could* or not didn't really matter. After Mikasa's and Elijah's lame attempts, they'd given up. Jasper was just glad to have someone in his corner again, and he'd all but forgotten about his own stalkerish actions of last night.

"What about work?" Jasper asked. "Don't they need you?"

"Screw work." Finn took his cell from his pocket and held it up to his ear. "This is far more important. *You* are more important."

Jasper couldn't hold back his smile. It had been years since he'd felt so damn special.

"Hey, Gabriel, it's me." Finn turned away and began to pace around the apartment, weaving in and out of Jasper's belongings. "Did you get my notes? Good, good."

Then Finn shot him a pointed look of surprise, and Jasper was confused until he realized he'd been so shocked by Finn's visit that he'd forgotten to cover up the piece he was working on, and during his conversation, Finn had gone over to study it.

Jasper almost had a heart attack as he ran across the room and fetched the tarp to conceal it.

"I've got something to take care of, so I'm going to be late today," Finn said, keeping Jasper at arm's length so he couldn't cover it up. Frowning, he made a disgruntled noise at the cell call. "None of your business, Gabe."

When Finn silenced the conversation with a click, mortification flushed Jasper's cheeks.

"This is… um," Finn stalled. He looked like he was either about to laugh or cry. "Racy…."

Jasper had no choice but to own the moment. "I get bored easily. This is the closest thing I've had to a sexual experience in months."

Finn bellowed with laughter and playfully punched Jasper on the arm. When he calmed down, he rotated the easel into the light to inspect it further. "He's a pretty good-looking dude."

Jasper's heart fell into his stomach, and he would have laughed too, were he not so stunned. He presumed Finn already knew.

"Hang on a sec," Finn whispered. "Is this… it's… me?"

If somebody could ever have died of shame, it would've been Jasper in that very moment.

Finn looked from him to the painting, the painting to him. When Jasper nodded for confirmation, Finn put his face right up to the genitals. They were the first thing Jasper had mapped out, and it only looked strange in comparison to the rest of the piece because he'd tried to finish them first to allow the layers to dry.

"Jesus Christ, Jasper!" Finn was half smiling, half cringing. "What a shocking and… generous imagination you have."

Smiling to himself, Jasper went to fix a coffee and left an astonished Finn to admire the nude portrait of himself.

Of late, things had been confusing as hell. One thing was for certain, though. Jasper was practically itching to know just how accurate he'd been with his phallic estimations.

JASPER HAD no idea what happened to Finn either last night or this morning, but it meant a great deal that Finn was being so kind, and he held a lot of stock in Jasper's meager abilities. Whatever switch had been flicked in Finn's brain, he seemed to believe Jasper was going to play a big part in his future.

Which could maybe even be *their* future.

Exciting as that was, Jasper foresaw complications working with Finn if he ever got out of that damned apartment, but he tried to shove the doubt aside and paste on a smile.

He wanted to spend as much time with Finn as possible, but he didn't know if that was because of Finn himself, or because he hadn't had sex in so long and he was itching for the slightest bit of intimacy. Either way, the tension between them was obvious as they spent a good portion of the afternoon on the couch poring over more ancient tomes.

"This is absolute insanity," Finn said. "Look here."

Finn set his cup on the coffee table and the book between them and leaned into Jasper. Finn smelled of sandalwood and musk, and Jasper edged closer.

How much had Finn thought about last night's kiss? Did he regret it, or were they moments away from recreating it? Jasper was so aware of Finn's proximity that he had a hard time focusing on the words he pointed to and began to read aloud.

"Beings who sustain magical properties are susceptible to prolonged periods of rumination. It is in their constitution to look inward when complications arise, and occasionally, when matters become truly arduous, it is not uncommon for the typical mage to feel entombed beneath his own influence."

"Wow." Jasper was both ecstatic to learn something new and because Finn gripped his thigh in excitement. His reading voice was hot as hell, and it would've been easy to sit for hours listening to him read the whole volume. "That's... awesome."

Finn nodded his head in agreement. "I know. Means we might stand a chance of getting you out of here after all."

"Yeah," Jasper muttered. He tried to play it cool, as if this news weren't the best thing he'd heard in months. And yet, he was also of two minds. "Seems like you're trying very hard to get me free. While I appreciate it... anyone else might think you were just using me for my gift. That you don't want to spend real time with me. Hey, I guess it's a good thing I'm not an insecure psycho who jumps to conclusions or anything...."

Apparently unconvinced, Finn arched an eyebrow and gave Jasper a pointedly long stare while he chewed the inside of his mouth. "I don't mean to lay it on too thick this early on, but I want you to listen to me carefully. I would never use you for personal gain. Manipulation of any form isn't my style—I prefer being up-front. And in the interest of honesty, I simply want you to be your happiest self. All I'm trying to do is double my chances of making that happen by offering two ways of letting your genius orbit around me. It can't hurt to try, eh?"

Nodding slowly, Jasper found himself a little choked up. Though he was well versed in the complications of color, from time to time, he also enjoyed things painted in black and white. Finn offered refreshing clarity and a distinct lack of mind games compared to all of Jasper's exes.

"What's say we strike a deal?" Finn laid a hand flat on Jasper's thigh.

"Oh?"

"Every time we stumble across a new revelation about your predicament, you practice that wonderful ability of yours. Start thinking of ways for our partnership to blossom."

By way of answer, Jasper offered a toothy grin. "That seems fair. And thanks for putting me at ease. Sometimes reassurance does me a world of good." Jasper covered Finn's hand with one of his own. "Do I get to negotiate some terms too?"

Finn tilted his head to the side and locked his gaze. Jasper found their exchange all very amusing, and he was willing to bet that, through all his boardroom meetings, there was no chance Finn had ever struck a deal inches away from a man whose lust was virtually perfuming the air.

"Every time you get that look in your eye," said Jasper, "I'm free to practice my other… abilities. I'm quite gifted in those areas too, by the way. And you're more than welcome to use me for personal gain in that respect."

Though Finn's mouth popped open with surprise, he managed a hitched "Okay."

So Jasper leaned forward and planted his mouth on Finn's and kissed him with reckless abandon.

Finn's lips were as soft as Jasper remembered. His mouth tasted of sweet coffee, and that lovely sandalwood clung to his stubble. Even though they hadn't known each other long, Jasper was beyond ready to take their connection to the next level.

He sparked a bolt of lust in Jasper that he hadn't felt in years, and it didn't take long for him to climb up on Finn's lap and root his hands in his hair as he explored Finn's mouth with his tongue.

"Fuck," Finn breathed. With one hand he supported Jasper's neck while he planted the other firmly on his back, securing him in place. "Your eagerness is such a turn-on."

"Is it?" Jasper whispered, trying to keep the feeling of desperation from oozing out of his pores. "Can I?"

"Yeah," Finn spoke, grinning into the kiss.

As he slowly began to grind his hips, Finn's dick got halfway hard. Jasper didn't need more confirmation than that.

Pulling the shirt over his head, he moaned as Finn kissed his nipples. It was incredible to have his cool breath on such a sensitive place, and Jasper was in a frenzy as he climbed off his lap and shimmied out of his pants. Finn's eyes were fixed on his boxer shorts, and more specifically, the bulge protruding from them.

But this moment was about Finn and Jasper's innate need to satisfy him.

Getting down on his knees, he hooked his hands on to Finn's belt and popped the metal. In one swoop he had the leather in his hands and tossed it aside. Finn undid his flies and yanked the fabric all the way down. Jasper had no doubt the gray Ralph Laurens cost a bomb, but he didn't care as he ripped them off. Finn's cock was the goal, and Jasper was beside himself when he freed it from the cotton prison and found that he had underestimated his size.

If they were in a forest and not on his couch, the thing could easily be mistaken for a Burmese python.

"Wow," Jasper breathed, gazing in awe at the bulbous head peeking out from a generous amount of foreskin. It was a feast for the eyes, and Jasper didn't know what to appreciate first.

His balls hung low between his thighs, and the whole region was perfectly manscaped with what must've been exactly half an inch of pubic hair. It was clear Finn took pride in himself, and Jasper didn't wait any second longer to pull the foreskin back and dive in.

"Oh…. Oh my God," Finn moaned as he was taken to the base.

His dick was where it belonged as it stretched Jasper's throat, and he could already taste the sweetness of silky precum. It was empowering to see sheer ecstasy on the face of a powerful man with his head tilted back, taking what he wanted in the name of pleasure.

With Finn's hand firmly planted in Jasper's hair, moving him exactly where he wanted as he thrust up from below, it wasn't long before they got into a good rhythm, and even though Jasper's own dick was stiffer than a tentpole, he jerked it with care. He wanted the moment to last.

"You like that?" Jasper asked when he came up for air, eyeing the reaction as he grazed Finn's shaft with the tip of his tongue.

"Very much," Finn said, bending down for a kiss. "You weren't kidding about being talented."

Jasper giggled into the kiss, but when Finn tried to pull him up, he pushed back and returned to his knees. "No, no," he said. "This is all for you. Let me take care of you."

"Hmm," Finn grumbled. But it was hard to refuse pleasure when Jasper took him in to the base again and Finn's tip touched his tonsils.

Luckily, Jasper's knew a neat trick to avoid triggering his gag reflex, and he would gladly suck Finn for hours on end if it meant he could keep that delicious musky scent in the back of his nose.

"Can we at least go to the bed?" Finn breathed, fingers resolutely wound through Jasper's hair. "That way I can touch you too."

"Fine," Jasper conceded, but it made sense to bring the action to the sheets.

Licking his lips, Jasper stayed put on the couch to get a shameless view of Finn's ass as he got up. He wanted a better vantage point than when he'd spied on him before, but apparently, Finn wasn't having any of it.

"Come here, you," Finn ordered. When he ducked down to scoop Jasper into his arms as though he weighed no more than a pumpkin, Jasper was thankful for the grueling workouts he'd witnessed through Finn's window.

He cried out with surprise at the manhandling, but it took all of two seconds for him to realize that the skin-on-skin contact was something his body was very much craving.

Finn planted a firm kiss on Jasper's mouth as he carried him to the bedroom. When they got to the foot of the bed, Jasper was expecting to be let down, but he was lost in the moment.

"Oh shit," Jasper cried as he was sent flying to the bed. Then Finn jumped on top of him and rubbed his length across Jasper's torso. He was a playful lover.

Latching his lips right back onto Jasper's, Finn grunted softly as he pillaged Jasper's mouth with his tongue, the line between need and comfort completely blurred.

Jasper moaned into Finn and raked his fingernails across his back.

"Can I take care of you too?" Finn asked, voice dripping with need.

Jasper was about to protest, but he realized the importance of equality. It was hard to believe they truly desired each other in equal measures... yet maybe it was the truth. He could feel himself a few minutes away from exploding, and he began to worry about it being less than awe inspiring.

"Sure," he agreed, chuckling as Finn did a one-eighty, then guided his cock back into Jasper's waiting mouth as he sunk his lips around Jasper's.

Finn's warm, wet tongue was flat against his cut shaft as he mimicked Jasper's actions by taking him to the max. If Jasper had been at all worried about feeling inadequate next to Finn's formidable physique, Finn's devoted attention burned away any lingering doubt. Jasper was often the giver, not the receiver, and he wondered why that was when it felt so fucking good. It was natural to sixty-nine this way. To be skull-fucked by Finn as he jackhammered his head up and down.

When Jasper's thighs began to tremble, he knew his orgasm was looming. Using both hands, he jerked Finn fiercely to the point where his balls started to tighten. They were still big enough to be able to slap at Jasper's nose and perfume the air with that delicious musky scent.

"Oh God," Jasper garbled a moan, beginning to quake, seconds away from painting Finn's face white.

"Yeah?" Finn asked, voice husky as he fisted his shaft over and over. "Come for me, Jasper. Please."

Jasper did as he was asked, brain turning to pulp when he reached for the stars and lost all sense of being. As he let loose pump after pump, Finn let out a carnal roar when he let himself go too, and Jasper filled Finn's mouth with a warm reward.

"Damn," Finn groaned, using his hand to milk the last of his load into Jasper's mouth.

Jasper swallowed and couldn't keep the giggle in as he licked up the remnants of Finn's orgasm like a hot fudge sundae.

When he came back to face Jasper, something had changed. Now that they had shared intimacies, there was no going back. A bond had been forged between them, and he couldn't remember a time when he'd been so excited to explore something new.

When Finn kissed his forehead and let Jasper rest on his pecs, he breathed a deep, contented sigh. Maybe the whole world wasn't out to get him after all.

CHAPTER ELEVEN

FINN COULDN'T remember the last time he'd had sex even half as good as that. And they'd only gone as far as oral.

Their exchange was raw, needy, and filled with emotion and promise—pretty much the exact opposite of everything he'd come to expect.

Finn couldn't recall the last time someone had made him feel as wanted as Jasper had, and it was liberating to be more than just a tool in a mutual orgasm. Theirs had been an equal trade.

"I *cannot* wait to do that again." Finn spoke to the ceiling. Stroking Jasper's hair as he lay on his chest, Finn was surprised it wasn't the slightest bit awkward to have an effective stranger so close. "Might have to give it a while, though," he added. "You've well and truly worn me out. I'm seconds from slipping into a satisfaction coma."

Jasper's breath fell hot on Finn's body where he laughed heartily. He peppered a few kisses along Finn's torso and then propped himself up and allowed Finn to continue absently looping his hair around his fingers.

"If I didn't know any better...." Jasper tickled Finn's abs. "I'd swear you only like me for my old-fashioned golden locks."

"That's simply not true," said Finn, pretending to be offended even though, among Jasper's features, they were definitely one of his favorites. Gazing at him, even in the postsex haze, it was easy for Finn to appreciate Jasper's striking beauty. He'd never come across anyone who could balance boyish, clean features with a mannish, veiny, muscled look. Normally Finn went for twig-thin twinks who could bend themselves into a pretzel, but Jasper had a little bit of meat on him, and he was cool with that.

"I like your stubble," Finn said, running a finger along Jaspers jaw, "and your cute little button nose." When Finn poked Jasper's nose, Jasper rolled his eyes. "Your feet are hairier than a hobbit's... but who likes feet anyway? Mine are stubby like a goblin's, so we're at least in the same book if not on the same page. Plus, you have those bottomless ultramarine eyes and an ass to die for."

Leaning back, Jasper seemed undecided. He was probably making up his mind whether to take the compliments or linger on the foot one.

"What do you like about me?" Finn couldn't help fish for a compliment since he'd just baited the air.

"You have a really fat cock."

"That's it?" Finn pinched his arm. "That's all you can think of?"

"Currently? Yes." Jasper dove down under the covers to scatter light kisses along Finn's hypersensitive balls. "I suppose your nuts are nice too."

"Thanks."

Rearing his head, Jasper winked. "I know you're worn out, but maybe you could find the strength to pull through and have breakfast with me?"

"Sure, absolutely," Finn agreed, rising to meet Jasper's level. "That sounds great."

It was pretty disconcerting for Finn to have sex with someone and *then* get to know them. But he knew that he wanted to. Pure magnetism had gotten them to this point, and the thought of munching on another one of Jasper's amazing concoctions spurred Finn to find out more.

But before they could do any of that, Finn had to do something about the postsex smell.

"Is it all right if I take a quick shower before I join you?"

"Be my guest," Jasper said, sweeping a hand toward the bathroom. "Towels are in the antique cabinet. Well, I say antique... I probably paid a premium for some student to batter and scratch it up."

Grinning, Finn climbed off the bed.

"Don't start cooking without me." Finn gave his own ass a cheeky slap as he walked away, knowing full well Jasper was staring at it.

"Wouldn't dream of it," Jasper called as he entered the bathroom.

Where Finn's bathroom matched the rest of his minimalist apartment, Jasper's was full of personality. Three potted plants were crammed onto the vintage cabinet he'd spoken of, the shelves were lined with nautical-themed trinkets, a signpost stating *Love Life* was drilled into the checkered tiles, and the shower curtain was a curious blend of yellow polka dot and white beach sand. It was mismatched and nonsensical—everything he had come to learn about Jasper over the last few days.

Letting the shower run for a minute, Finn checked himself out in the mirror. His hair was a complete mess, his eyes were bloodshot, and there were fingernail marks on his shoulders where Jasper had gripped him. He'd never looked so run-down in his entire life, and yet he'd never felt so utterly satisfied.

By the time he jumped in the shower, he was already starting to think of gifts to buy for Jasper, but he didn't yet know enough about him besides their fatal attraction.

"Finn?" Jasper's voice filtered through the door. "Is the screen drawn all the way?"

"Um, yes?" Finn said. "Why?

"Just…," he muttered, "make sure it is. I'm dying to take a leak."

Before he could so much as think of a protest, the door creaked open and Jasper's silhouette appeared on the other side of the curtain.

Finn froze in place. Thankfully the water pressure was so loud that he didn't hear Jasper going about his business, and he knew Jasper was done when he pulled the chain and the water went ice-cold for just a moment.

"Peekaboo!" Jasper pulled back the curtain, and Finn almost fell out of the bath from surprise. "Nice hair, stud."

No doubt it was sky-high and full of soapy suds, but he was more focused on keeping his hands fixed over his privates. He didn't know why he was so embarrassed considering all they had just done. Not to mention the fact that Jasper himself was still stark naked.

"Well, I'll leave you to it." He winked and then dragged the curtain back and made a leisurely exit.

When Finn got over his daze, he shook his head and laughed through his nose. Clearly Jasper had a lot of pent-up energy... but damn, boundary issues could be an issue if Finn let them.

This was the fastest roller coaster of his life, and it shocked Finn to the core that he didn't plan to get off anytime soon.

CHAPTER TWELVE

"I PUT some Febreze on your clothes," Jasper said when Finn walked out, hair still damp and with a towel wrapped around his waist.

Jasper got an eyeful as Finn dropped the cloth, let everything hang out, and started to put his suit back on. "Thanks. I appreciate that."

"Maybe go a bit slower?" Jasper asked, leaning his elbows on the counter and forgetting all about the ingredients. "I think we may have enough time for round two before you leave."

"Do you, now?" Finn smirked and shook on his shirt, allowing his rippling abs to peek between the folds. "My legs would turn to jelly before I could go into work."

"Okay, okay." Reluctantly, Jasper turned his attention back to breakfast. "How do you like your eggs? Sunny-side up or over easy?"

"How about poached?" Finn took a seat on a barstool and watched Jasper arrange raw eggs with a slab of bread dough and uncooked bacon. "Just wanted to test your limits is all. Also, have you ever heard of cross contamination?"

Hovering his hands over the plate, energy started to thrum beneath Jasper's skin. "It doesn't apply. Now shush."

Closing his eyes, Jasper focused on the fibers woven into the DNA of the food. He pictured them in their current organic state, worthless to humans. But when he pictured that DNA after an imaginary heat had been applied, he knew exactly what his end goal was, and the items before him were cooked to perfection as though he'd ripped them from the pages of a Thomas Keller cookbook.

"Amazing," Finn commented as he leaned forward and drank in the heavenly concoction of aromas. He licked his lips as Jasper handed him some cutlery and watched him dig in. "Aren't you having some?"

"Nah," said Jasper. He used to have an appetite healthier than Finn's, but ever since he got trapped, he only ate two times a day. He had no way to get proper exercise besides jumping jacks.

"What's on the agenda today, then?" Finn asked between bites. "Are you going to keep capturing my essence on that canvas?"

"Absolutely," Jasper said. "And, for the hundredth time, I'll probably research how I ended up here. For all it's worth."

With his mouth full, Finn hummed his appreciation. "Maybe you could think of a way to blend your magic with my work while I'm gone?"

"I can try…." Though he was keen to help, Jasper didn't want to get in the habit of making empty promises.

But he could promise to always enjoy every single time he kissed Finn. And when Finn finished his breakfast, Jasper made sure to give him a big kiss he would remember all day.

THE SURPRISE visit from Finn had settled Jasper's doubt, and he was positively giddy as he spent the rest of the morning and half the afternoon painting. Since he was illustrating Finn in the buff, it seemed fitting for Jasper to paint in the nude. Freeing his hair from its band, he grabbed a freshly cleaned brush and got to work on layer number thirty-four.

While this particular piece would be his pick of the bunch, Jasper was spending an embarrassingly long time perfecting the curve of Finn's member because he couldn't nail the wrist action needed to get the depth required. His realism role model, Edward Hopper, would probably be disappointed.

Though he preferred the Alla Prima technique for abstract works because he could complete a perfectly passable still life in one sitting, Jasper's penchant for intricate portraits forced him to employ the Glazing technique, where he had to paint in small bursts and let each layer dry before proceeding with the next.

Stepping back, Jasper wondered if he could blast the canvas with a hairdryer on Low to speed up the process.

"Whatever," he sighed. "Can't rush perfection."

Not only did the method eat up time that could be better spent, but the fat-over-lean rule of thumb also meant the arrangement was more of an optical illusion since the pigments never actually mixed, and the canvas would begin to crack if Jasper didn't pay close attention to the oil content of his next layer and study the translucent quality of his paints.

Between drying time, Jasper varnished a few of his most recent pieces and switched the order of them on the gesso rack by the window to allow for the most airspace given his unusual predicament. He then settled on getting in sweatpants, snacking on a bowl of freshly magicked mac and cheese as he whiled the day away researching more on his entrapment.

It didn't take long for the words on the brittle pages to start blending into an amalgam of inescapable doom, so Jasper tried to take Finn's suggestion and think of something worthwhile.

Maybe he could throw some food on canvases and utilize his gift in that way? But that seemed a little too abstract for Jasper's style. Or maybe he could paint with the guts of the foodstuffs he'd enhanced. No, that wouldn't work either.

When something else occurred to Jasper, he faceplanted on the couch. Now he knew what Finn felt like when he called himself dumb. The answer had been right in front of his face all this time.

Grabbing a cookbook at random, Jasper flipped to the bread section and found himself gaping at the intricate baskets people had handwoven before baking. He could definitely do that with his gift. And if he could do that, what was stopping him getting more creative? Why stop at bread? Why not make statues out of cake and elaborate towers out of french fries? The possibilities were endless, and as Jasper morphed egg rolls into a sort of bridge shape, he had to ground himself for a minute.

He needed a theme. A purpose.

Finn had yet to share his company's true goal, so Jasper was in the dark in that respect. What would the people buying these sculptures appreciate most?

Jasper would have to be smart with his selection of ingredients to come up with a demonstratable piece. It would be magicked together, obviously, but it had to be made from a convincing enough foundation if the humans were to believe he'd handmade it.

Without Finn's further guidance, Jasper left his piece on the counter, scribbled some notes on a pad, and shelved the idea for later.

Fed up, he buried himself with his comforter on the couch and settled on reading up on astral projection. Some things weren't worth pushing for. In time, he would find the correct headspace to ponder his next venture.

Just as Jasper was delving deep into physical-versus-metaphysical touch, three loud knocks banged on the front door.

Startled, he dropped the bowl of food onto the floor and set the book aside. Carefully angling a tarp over his painting, Jasper combed his hands through his hair, opened the door, and almost went into cardiac arrest.

"Oh Gods, Jasper!" In walked Jasper's mom, brushing past him in a fur coat without so much as a smile, nose pinched by two fingers. "It reeks in here."

"Mom," Jasper cried, shutting the door. "How did you...? When did you—"

"Honestly, Jasper. This place is in a dreadful state. Can't you open a window?"

Instead of pausing for a breath, she took it upon herself to go over and crank open the bay window as far as it would go. Then she picked up his clothes and tossed them in the washing bin.

"I can't put my hand outside," Jasper said. "Or *go* outside, for that matter."

She pointed to the edible arrangement he'd been practicing on. "How long has that monstrosity of an excuse for food been sitting there rotting away?"

"That's my new project. Please don't touch it. And didn't you hear me?" Jasper's mom had always had her own agenda, but it was pretty clear she was actively avoiding him. "I'm trapped here."

"Never mind that." She waved a hand, taking off her coat and getting to work piling his cups into the sink. "What's the dating situation like? When are you going to find yourself a wealthy husband?"

"Mom, we've been through this *so* many times."

"We have?" she asked, gathering more stuff, pretending not to remember the countless times Jasper had refuted her pushiness, insisting he make his own way in life. But she seemed to find the very notion of him standing on his own feet impossible.

"I swear I'd get more sense talking to the wall."

"Don't make me use my gift on you, son. It's been years since I took the vow to never do that."

Jasper did know. And he also knew that she would never actually do it—it was just an idle threat that was her way of saying she was legitimately angry.

Instead of standing there vacuously, Jasper helped tidy too. "I've actually met someone," he said. "Someone I actually like and see a future with, believe it or not."

With her lips firmly pursed, Jasper's mom was silent for a full minute. It was delightful.

"When he fails on you, I've got the perfect man lined up. You've already been there once, mind, but he's a changed man now, and I'm certain it will work out this time."

Jasper shook his head and bit his tongue. It wasn't worth the argument to point out that he was about halfway to officially dating Finn, and the sexy businessman was turning out to be Jasper's perfect match. Jasper's mom had met Jasper's dad back in wizard college when they were twelve, so of course her life had been a picture-perfect romance. She really needed to give up on the idea that his would be too.

"How long are you in town for?" Jasper wondered, eager to shift topics. "Is Dad here too?"

Though he had brought it up, Jasper's spine tingled at the thought of seeing his father again. Wherever he was, he'd no doubt be wearing his vintage leather jacket and he would complain about Jasper's unruly hair compared to his easy-to-maintain buzzcut. Of course Jasper looked like shit. It had been months since he'd stepped foot in a salon.

"It's just me for now," Jasper's mom said. "Your father had to take care of business back home while I came here to look for somebody who can make Sara's wedding cake."

Her words were like a literal slap in the face. Not only did she not come here to check up on his welfare, but she was busy looking for someone to cater his sister's wedding cake when Jasper could do it at the click of a finger. Not to mention he'd worked in a handful of bakeries.

Rather than shout and verbally dance around in circles with her, Jasper dove into the fridge, assembled some ingredients into a pan, and waved his hands over them. Closing his eyes, warmth buzzed through his flesh, and he heard the ingredients meld. When he opened his eyes, a three-tiered fruit cake with marzipan and white icing sat before him. He had even made two edible sculpture toppers.

"Well?" Jasper said, eager for his mom's stony façade to crack just a little and give away any sort of feeling. "Imagine what I could make if I actually gave it some thought? Though if the wedding is soon, somebody will have to come back here and transport it…."

"You know the rules, honey," Jasper's mom said, intent on scrubbing dishes even though Jasper could hear them squeaking under the water. "We don't keep business in the family. Never have, never will."

"Are you serious?" Jasper's lid had well and truly blown off. "I might as well not *be* a part of this so-called family. You act like you have my best interest at heart, but all you care about is yourself and the social ladder you're desperate to climb."

"Now, Jasper," his mom said, drying her hands on the towel just so she could place them on her hips. "There's no need to be rude. Let's have a cup of coffee and talk about this."

"No," said Jasper, backing up to retrieve her coat. "I'd like you to leave."

As her face pinched in on itself, she looked like someone had slapped her with a rotten fish. She was plainly affronted, and she could barely form words.

"Well," she stuttered. "I don't wish to. You wouldn't cast your own mother out."

Jasper whistled through his teeth, knowing exactly where he got his stubbornness. "It's not like I can leave, so please don't subject me to this torture any longer."

"You're not serious."

Jasper sniggered drily. "I assure you that I am. You haven't listened to a word I've said since you arrived, and I don't want to raise my voice at you, mother. Please just go."

Huffing and muttering to herself, Jasper's mom took a moment longer to let the hurt settle in before her bold façade reared its head again and she acted like she didn't care one bit as she yanked her coat from him and stormed out of the apartment.

CHAPTER THIRTEEN

AS SOON as the watch on his wrist stroked five o'clock, Finn was out of the building. As he strode out of the dank subway in search of caffeine, he couldn't wait to get back to Jasper.

Standing in line gave Finn pause from the echoes of four separate investment meetings bumbling around his brain. Thinking of more intimate contact with Jasper turned out to be Finn's light in the dark, and he wanted to reward him—both for being unapologetically himself and for the amazing blowjob he'd given Finn.

"Excuse me, sir?" someone called. "Sir? Can I help you?"

Finn stopped examining the skillfully frosted almond-jam tarts. "Sorry, miles away. I'll have an Americano and a vanilla latte please."

As the barista prepared his order, Finn's mind raced with possibilities. He wanted to surprise Jasper with something special, something small and meaningful to complement his dual nature.

With cups in hand, Finn took a detour to Jasper's place and darted into a renowned jewelry store. He already had something pictured in his mind's eye, but when he glossed over glitzy rings and overly feminine necklaces, he found the ideal gift in a little cabinet all to itself. It was a thick bracelet woven from interlocking bands of titanium that tapered gradually to form a clasp laced with midnight black pearls. Finn's head almost fell off when he saw the price tag, but it was too perfect to pass up. Not only was it a modest token to celebrate Finn's recent emotional revelation, Jasper might actually be able to put it to use with his magic.

A few minutes later, Finn left the store with a classy gift bag and a hefty dent in his bank account. For a while now, Finn knew his father had been monitoring his expenditures. But screw it. Jasper's happiness had no price, and he would suffer the argument later on.

Finn decided against using the elevator in Jasper's building. He'd been slacking on gym time lately, so even though there was a risk of spilling hot coffee on himself, he squeezed a quick workout in by trotting up the snaking stairway.

When he neared Jasper's apartment, a middle-aged woman was standing outside his place, mumbling to herself angrily as she struggled to shrug on a fur coat.

Leaning on the doorframe, she whipped out her cell, and whatever was on it only served to add to her exceptionally perturbed expression. Standing there awkwardly with a gift bag in one hand and the cup holder in the other, Finn couldn't get past without talking to her.

"Hi," he said, waiting for her to finish furiously tapping. "Are you coming or going?"

Finn already knew the answer—he was trying to be polite.

She locked her phone, stuffed it into her pocket, and eyed him as she peeled herself from the doorframe. "Leaving, apparently. That child of mine is a headache sometimes."

"You're Jasper's mother?"

"Yes." She arched a thinly penciled brow. "Who's asking?"

"Nobody," said Finn. "Just a friend."

The way she was looking at him set Finn on edge. He couldn't remember what power Jasper had claimed she had, but there was no question as to whether she was sizing him up. It had probably taken her all of two seconds to scope out the fact he was human.

"You know," she continued, "I'm surprised he still has friends, the way he acts."

Hurt on Jasper's behalf, Finn decided to be bold. "You know he's trapped in there, right?"

"Well, yes, of course I know that," she said, staring at him, confused. "How do *you* know that? Don't tell me he's told you...."

"About his abilities?" Finn finished, watching sheer disbelief mar her face. "Yeah."

She wouldn't stop shaking her head in disapproval, even as she spoke. "Stars above. I warned him time and time again the repercussions of breaking our code. How did I produce such a naïve son?" As she stared through him, it was clear she wasn't looking for an answer. "And why is it you think I'm here?" She might've expected a response. "That boy just *doesn't* understand I'm trying to push him out of this tangle."

With her tendency to speak rhetorically, Finn guessed she could probably be more direct with Jasper. Apparently finished with the conversation, she made a move to turn away. But Finn wasn't done.

Shuffling the cups and gift bag into one hand, she jerked when he put his other hand on her arm. "But you do want what's best for him, right?"

Looking from the hand back to Finn, she narrowed her eyes to slits. "Obviously."

"Then why not help him?" The grip on her arm tightened as Finn couldn't help himself grow bothered. It was too similar to exactly how his parents had been treating him. "If you know how to get him free, why prolong his agony?"

"Kindly remove yourself from me, or I'll force your hand." The fire in her eyes was not to be tested. Finn apologized and put his hand back at his side, not knowing what had come over him. "Quite the outburst over *just a friend*, wouldn't you say? Oh my. Don't tell me you're the one he's dating?" She looked him up and down, apparently not liking what she saw. "Heavens. I knew my child was rebellious, but *this*? This is something else entirely."

As she continued to study his every feature, Finn took a moment's pause. If Jasper's parents were, in fact, similar to his own, there was every reason they were hard on him for the same reasons. They both wanted their sons to succeed.

"It goes against code to help him directly," she said, getting out a pocket mirror to check that her pristine bob haircut was still in place. "There's little point me telling you this, really. You two can't last. But maybe you do have some use for the time being. If there's any developments in my absence, call me." From her pocket, she withdrew a black business card with the name *Evangeline Wight* embossed with gold lettering. "I'm late for a meeting."

As she scurried to the elevator without a second glance, Finn breathed a sigh of relief. The very pressure in the air lifted. Though he didn't know exactly what she had against him, at least now he knew where Jasper got his passion.

It was hard to believe that woman had made such a sweet son.

"FOR GOD'S sake!" came shouting through the door. "I thought I told you to ge—"

Jasper stopped short when he realized it was Finn, not his mother. "Only me," Finn said, giving him a kiss on the cheek before brushing past.

"Sorry." Jasper was visibly happy to receive his coffee. Before he went back to the kitchen to continue preparing dinner, he took a sip and it seemed to visibly calm him down. "My mom was just here, throwing her weight around."

"I just saw her outside."

"You met my mom?"

"Yeah. She's, uhh, interesting? She mostly talked *at* me instead of *to* me."

"That's kinda her thing." Jasper rolled his eyes. "She's never been this cold and distant. I mean, she's always been aloof, but it's gotten worse since I got trapped. Beats me. She also loves a bit of mage-human prejudice."

"Oh," Finn gasped. "That's why she was looking at me like I'd grown two heads? Can she sense that I'm not one of yours or something?"

When Jasper nodded gently, an apology was written in his eyes. "Did she manage to talk about anything but herself?"

Finn shrugged, unsure how to proceed. Jasper's mom had imparted some useful knowledge, and it felt weird to keep it to himself. And yet, if what she said was true, that Jasper had to figure out how do it alone, that it was a journey of self-discovery, filling Jasper's head with information Finn knew little about might only serve to endanger him further.

If he wasn't careful, Finn could undo Jasper's progress and set him back double the number of months he'd already spent holed up. He probably wouldn't appreciate that very much.

In the spirit of keeping his best interest at heart, it was probably better for Finn to keep quiet.

CHAPTER FOURTEEN

WHEN YOU'RE getting to know somebody, silence can be an incredible bonding exercise. If it continues to feel awkward to be silent in someone's presence, something's up. Fortunately, Finn passed that test with flying colors, and twenty minutes of nothing but pure, affectionate snuggling did Jasper's soul a world of good. It felt good to be wanted again.

"How's about that dinner, then?" Finn stroked Jasper's chin. "Work was draining enough on top of that workout we had this morning."

"All right," Jasper agreed, grinning. "We need something calorie heavy, in that case. What does beef casserole sound like?"

"Very British," Finn joked. "But very wonderful."

"I get inspired by all types of art from around the world." Jasper headed back to the kitchen, grateful that he had done most of the prep work earlier. "Food from France, paintings from Italy, history from Egypt."

Finn got up from the couch and edged around the seemingly all-purpose coffee table and a canvas-drying rack to watch Jasper work. "You must get so bored in here all alone. I can't imagine spending a *week* cramped up in my apartment."

"Cramped?" Jasper repeated. "In your place? Your living room is easily five times the size of this."

"Still," Finn said. "You deserve a medal for staying sane."

"That's probably the understatement of the year." Jasper laughed. "But I don't really mind that I don't have a television or anything.

Wasn't much of a couch potato before I got trapped, so I can't exactly miss it."

When Jasper opened the fridge to fetch ingredients, Finn grunted. "Is that thing even on?"

"Nope. And it doesn't need to be."

After throwing some very questionable-looking meat into the pot, Jasper tried to be sly about selecting vegetables with the least amount of fuzz on them. But Finn noticed.

"Uhm," he started, "do you expect me to eat those?"

"Fear not, Mr. Highbrow." Jasper winked. "They'll be just fine. Whatever state ingredients are in gets refreshed as though brand-new when I use my gift. It's become second nature by now for me to use it whenever I eat or drink something."

"That's neat," Finn commented. "And unbelievably useful."

"Right," Jasper sighed, unconvinced. His abilities were so commonplace to him that he was almost completely oblivious to their appeal. "But at least not using appliances for food saves on the electricity bill. Elijah was pretty happy about that."

"You know," Finn began, "I could foot the bill for a while if they aren't happy about paying for you."

Arching an eyebrow, Jasper continued to season the concoction with various stale herbs and wilted spices. Gastromancy didn't entirely call for them, and the order in which he used them made probably no sense at all to Finn, but the trained chef found himself in his element by putting on a show.

"I could never ask you to do that, Finn."

"You wouldn't have to," he said, eyeing the food as it bubbled up underneath Jasper's hands. "That's why I offered."

"Shush." When the stew had changed color from a gray tar-like substance to a thick auburn assortment that steamed and bubbled, wafting oodles of fresh aroma, Jasper went to the pan of vegetables and made them sizzle without the aid of any real heat. Their very DNA came back to life before Finn's eyes, and he wasn't quiet about expressing his fascination.

"Grub's up," Jasper announced as he spooned the medley into dishes and carried them to the couch.

As Finn took the first bite, his face spoke a thousand words. "Holy. Shit."

Jasper couldn't ask for a better compliment.

"So." Finn scratched his stubble and looked thoughtful. "I think we've reached that stage where I should know more about you. So, let's have it."

"Are you serious?" Jasper asked, scrunching his face. "It would take me at least a week to properly sort through my life in my own brain, let alone verbalize it in a nonmopey way."

"Well, I'm clearly in no rush to leave. I'm all ears." Finn rested a hand on Jasper's knee. "I promise I'll return the favor. We *could* save it for pillow talk… but I'd be all dreamy and distracted. I'd rather be alert and really hear what you've got to say."

Jasper was stumped. It was sweet that Finn was eager to learn about him, but he didn't much enjoy talking about himself. He'd learned to keep a wall up at all times, and it was difficult to take a sledgehammer to it just because Finn was asking him to.

But he knew this was a part of any normal bonding process. And he knew he needed another drink if they were to discuss heavy topics over dinner. Fortunately, the assortment of booze lining his kitchen cupboards rivaled the selection at Warehouse Wines on Broadway.

"Want some?" Jasper said, indicating an unopen bottle of pinot noir.

When Finn gave the universal why-not shrug, Jasper poured and brought two ridged tumblers back to the couch.

"Where should we start?" Jasper forked a potato. "At the most cliché part, I'd wager? When I realized I was gay?"

"Nah," Finn said. "Tell me about the time you knew you had magical powers."

Jasper almost choked on his food. "Finn, bud. You need to understand that's like me asking you to recall your time at kindergarten."

"Why? Because it's something you've always sort of known you had?"

When Jasper nodded, disappointment washed over Finn. He'd probably been hoping the mage had once had an awe-inspiring lightbulb moment where the world clicked into place.

Yeah, not so much.

"What was it like growing up?" Finn tried, ever persistent. "I bet it was pretty cool going to high school knowing you were secretly better than everyone around you."

Jasper let his jaw swing. "You think that's what it was like? Damn, Finn. I guess it's pretty good for the world *you* don't have powers with that kind of attitude."

Putting the wine back on the table, Finn surrendered his hands. "I meant no offense."

"I know you didn't," Jasper sighed, deliberately giving an awkward shoulder bump. "It's always been somewhat of a sore spot for me."

"How come?" Fin dug deeper. "I'm curious, is all. My upbringing was straight out of a Forbes weekly—strict parents, bullied from age eight, tried my hardest to build an empire. I imagine yours was a lot different, and I'm interested."

"Well yeah, I guess it was…." Jasper admitted. "My life began going down the shitter when I was six. Get the tissues ready," he said, finding a relatively clear spot to put the plates on the table. "I'm about to make you weep."

JASPER WAS saddened that Finn had been bullied, worse that he made the remark so casually. But it was clear he didn't want to talk about himself just yet. He wanted to learn about the history of a supernatural living in a human-governed world. So Jasper took a deep breath, put his food to one side, and tried to plan an explanation. In the interest of honesty, he wanted to be forthcoming. And yet he didn't want to scare Finn off.

"My sister, Sara, has the power of persuasion. She's three years younger than me, and even from an early age, she always got her way. Not just with my parents either. Getting the last donut or having a curfew later than mine was annoying, but even before she was taken to the regulations office for testing, she managed to skip class and get free candy from corner shops."

"Wow," Finn offered. "I always wondered what it would've been like growing up with siblings. Whether their constant influence would make me a better or worse person."

"Definitely the latter," Jasper laughed. "They're a royal pain in the ass. And not the fun kind! I grew to love her... but all of her success has eclipsed anything I've ever achieved in my life. When I was taken to the office for evaluation, my mom scoffed at the guy when he assessed my abilities. She made him study me three more times, and when it was evident that I did, in fact, have the gift of food manipulation, she didn't speak a word to me for a week."

"Shit." Finn drained his drink and went to get another one. Sensing the tone, he was smart enough to bring the bottle over. "And what is it your parents do?"

"Gift-wise? Mom can use tranquility at will, which is curious because I never felt anything but the exact opposite emotion around her." Jasper accepted another tumbler of wine, then clinked Finn's glass. "She's made it to a high advisory role with her talents, and every day she spends in that place, her web of lies gets bigger. I doubt they'd be able to recognize the real her if she took off her mask. But she's mastered the art of flying under the radar."

"That so?" Finn wondered. "What about those magisters you spoke of?"

"They only detect big rifts, remember? Her gift creates a ripple, not a tsunami. Sure, it might have the same effect in the end, over time, but the MRF doesn't much care, because it's subtle and effectively harmless. Our rules aren't like yours—it's less about not interfering in the nonmagical world and more about not exposing our kind."

Finn took that in and nodded slowly. "Super interesting. I would love to know just how many people in the public eye have abilities like that. Is there a way to find out?"

Jasper shrugged. "The British royal family is gifted. They're benevolent enough, though. Do better than bad, despite their riches. If they didn't, they wouldn't be allowed to keep their rule over humans. But sometimes I'm sure they dream of being normal just as I often do.

It would be nice to get where I want in life without the upper hand of some power that's been randomly bestowed on me for reasons I can scarcely comprehend. For me, it was almost like coming out twice. But I digress. My dad can shoot fireballs out of his hands, and last time I checked, he was working as an accountant, but he could be doing anything nowadays."

"What?" Finn was noticeably shocked. "He's got an ability as awesome as that and he's not putting it to use?"

"Well, yeah. His gift isn't subtle like mine or Mom's."

"Where are they living?"

"Rhode Island—my home state."

There was a smirk on Finn's face, and Jasper was quick to pinch his thigh and wipe it off. "Don't judge me. It's a homey little place."

"Hey." Finn caught the tumbler in his palm and held his hands up. "I come from Tulsa, the birthplace of Route 66 and world-renowned art museums."

"Don't you find it odd that most people in New York aren't actually from New York? Everything is so temporary these days."

"We're all seekers," Finn said. "People come here to make a name for themselves because it's the Paris of America."

"Is it really?" Jasper sipped his drink, relishing the slight dryness in his throat. "That's quite profound. Why have I never heard that before?"

"It's what I used to dream of when I was studying back in my petite box dorm. My French was never worth shit, so if I could move to the most romantic state in America, I might just get my fantasy."

"And did you? Correct me if I'm wrong… but I'm assuming you've been here a while. Your regional accent is barely noticeable. So," Jasper asked, more forcefully this time, "did you ever get your fantasy?"

"I'm starting to," Finn said. There was a fierce expression on his face, and Jasper couldn't work out what it was. Lust? Adoration? Distance? He wanted to lean in and kiss Finn, but the moment was gone.

"I hopped from job to job back home, trying to defy my predetermined calling, until I settled on being a chef," said Jasper. "I was always tucked away in the corner, hoping I could make it to head chef, but I never believed myself to be good enough. In spite of my gift, I wanted to learn the ropes the human way, because I enjoy the art of cookery. But when I did get better at my craft, the head chefs would earn Michelin stars and completely ignore the fact that the team—and largely me—had helped get it."

Finn nodded. "That must've been hard. You're incredibly talented. You should never have felt that way."

"But don't you see?" Jasper shot up. "I'm not talented in any way! The cooking thing is only an extension of this *gift* I've been given. I probably couldn't scramble an egg the way you could, with practice and care."

Finn's face wrinkled as the cogs turned in his brain. But Jasper wasn't done.

"If you could see the abilities of literally *any* other person in this city, you'd ridicule mine too. Just like my family. Just like everyone else I've encountered my entire life."

"Hey," Finn said, putting his drink down and pulling Jasper in so he could hold him tight and tuck some loose strands of hair behind his ear. "Stop being silly and start believing in yourself. We're going to get you out of this mess, and when we do, we're going to set up the best business in this place, and you'll get the recognition you deserve. Fuck your parents. And fuck my parents. Neither deserve us."

Jasper hadn't realized just how emotional he'd been feeling until Finn brushed away a loose tear. "This apartment is like a pressure can," he admitted. "All I want to do is get out on that street and breathe again. I'm a prisoner here. And I don't know what I've done to deserve it."

Finn didn't have any comforting words. He merely hugged Jasper tighter and let him fall into a relaxed space. And that was okay. He communicated everything that needed saying in that one piece of contact, and it felt like Jasper already knew Finn better than anyone he'd ever interacted with in the city.

"I know it's not the same, but have you tried projecting anywhere else than people's apartments?" Finn continued to run his fingers through Jasper's hair, making a new topknot. "Maybe if you found somewhere else to be in spirit, it might ease the feeling of loneliness."

"It's no use," Jasper sighed. "I can only project around someone I've made a connection with. And Mikasa's and Elijah's abilities are so strong, the interference meant I couldn't stand to be around them when I tried it with them. It was like sitting on every ride at Six Flags all at once with a pounding migraine."

"Interesting." Finn seemed lost in thought again, and it was touching to see how much he wanted to find a solution to Jasper's pain. "What are their abilities, exactly?"

"Stick around and you'll see."

That put a grin on his face. "And why the connection with me? I mean, how did you have that connection when I hadn't ever seen or spoken to you?"

"It works one-way too." Though he'd read up on it extensively, Jasper was tempted to tell Finn he didn't exactly have the handbook. "I made the connection myself when I got invested… in you."

He turned to look Finn dead in the eyes. Admitting something like that took a great deal of courage, and Jasper hoped Finn was able to read between the lines. He wanted them to be exclusive. The thought of him leaving the apartment to offer romantic visits to anyone else was painful.

"Pretty crazy, isn't it?"

Finn arched an eyebrow and looked from Jasper's eyes to his lips. "You don't need to tell me about crazy."

The kiss was imminent, and Jasper stretched out the moment of hesitation because he knew Finn was enjoying drinking him in. When Jasper finally took the bull by the horns, he grabbed the side of Finn's face and pulled him into a long, deep kiss. He was more confident with his moves by now, and as he brushed up against Finn, Jasper smiled when something hard poked out of his pants.

"Is there something in your pocket, or are you just happy to see me?"

Finn's jaw went slack for a moment, killing the vibe. Maybe he was embarrassed by his hard-on or he was trying to dodge sex altogether.

"There actually *is* something in my pocket," said Finn. When Jasper climbed off, Finn withdrew a small black box with a golden ribbon tied around it.

"What is that?"

"A gift," Finn said, "for you. Once again, I managed to get too distracted to remember I'd bought it."

Anticipation roiled Jasper's stomach. They hadn't known each other long enough for Finn to purchase some kind of unique gift.

"A while ago, I read somewhere that Merlin used to wear a silver bracelet because it helped him concentrate his aura… or something." Finn scratched the back of his neck. "I figured you deserved something similar."

When Finn opened the velveteen rectangle, he found a knitted band of metal of a bold yet intricate design, made from a brushed silvery metal that was peppered with dark opalescent gemstones.

Jasper couldn't wait a second longer to fix it onto his wrist.

"Do you like it?" Finn asked. "Not too feminine or anything?"

"It's breathtaking," Jasper admitted. "Just my style. But I feel bad now that I didn't get you anything. That I *can't* get you anything because I can't leave this damned place."

"Don't be silly." Finn put Jasper at ease with nothing but the soft touch of his lips on his. "Your company is the only prize I need."

Full of butterflies and hope, Jasper was a teenager again. "You can be pretty cute sometimes, Finn."

"Honestly," Finn breathed, "I don't know how I got so lucky."

"Probably because your parents worked hard to provide for you."

"I was talking about finding you, silly. Things have been less than peachy with my family for ages now."

"Tell me more," Jasper pleaded, drawing circles on his chest. "I want to hear about your past too."

"Well…," Finn paused. "If you could see us now, you'd think we've been used to wealth our entire lives. But there was a time my mom was anything but business-oriented. At age seven I was apparently old enough to look after myself, and while Dad was out brokering deals, she'd go to the arcade to bring back quarters and sift them into different bowls according to their rarity."

Jasper didn't know whether to laugh it off or bring Finn into another embrace. His tone suggested it wasn't an especially delightful tale, so Jasper listened carefully. He had the feeling straight-talking Finn didn't often share his story.

"I would go days without eating because she'd be examining those damn coins, convinced she'd find the big one at some point. 'I'm gonna get that lucky one someday soon, you'll see!' she'd say to me. 'Our life will be so much better, Finny!'" Finn shook his head and sighed. "I got that it was a kind of hobby of hers, but when I asked why I couldn't touch any of the heaping pile of rusted coins in the boiler room, she said she didn't want the coins going back in circulation in case she ended up getting them back herself."

"Wow," Jasper breathed. "Sounds like she's got quite an addictive personality."

"Pfft," Finn snarked. "That's putting it mildly. It was a bizarre thing for a child to be around at the time. I couldn't wrap my brain around the mindset for years, especially why my dad never put his foot down. But when she did eventually find a rare one and sold it on eBay, she cashed in all the other coins and bought a cute little water feature for herself and the latest Sega console to keep me happy. When she saw how much happier I was after actually getting three square meals a day, she got herself a nine-to-five the next week. She put so much faith into it, then she had a complete turnaround, and nobody has spoken of it since. Now *that's* crazy."

"Yeah, it kinda is." Jasper sensed it was safe enough to offer a small giggle. "But what matters is that her heart was in the right place. She wanted so desperately to provide a better life for you, and maybe the reason your parents push you so hard now is because they know you can succeed."

"Not going in their direction, I can't. It started as a passion project, but it's become too commercial. There's too much money involved."

"Hey, come to think of it, I've always wanted a man who's nouveau riche." Winking, Jasper tried to lighten the mood, but apparently the crease on Finn's brow was there to stay.

"We're actually more like old money than new money. It was my grandfather who initially earned our fortune, and my dad wasn't able to do anything with it until he took and ran with my idea of app-ordered subscription boxes. It's been almost a year since that function went live, and over five years since we sold a paper copy. It's pretty sad, but I guess he hopes more money will put him in better standing with the rest of the family. Working alongside you, though? Maybe we can succeed there."

Jasper cringed. "It's a lot of pressure, you know? To live up to expectations that I know you've already got in that head of yours. I don't want us to end up being at each other's throats if we become business partners."

"We won't. I promise."

That didn't do much to help quell Jasper's doubts. Finn had been in business for a long time, and he was going into this headfirst, knowing exactly what to expect. Jasper, on the other hand, had only stayed in one very easy lane.

"What kind of name would we even have for our project?" Jasper asked. "That would set the tone for the whole thing? I definitely like the idea of primarily making sculpture-like stuff—something grand and imposing. How about Fine Art Fancies?"

"Hmm." Finn turned up his nose. "It's a little banal."

"Jasper's Delights?" Nah. That sounded like too much like a seedy nightclub. "Oh, wait! How about Scrumptious Sculptures? I can make all of New York's monuments from fruit and vegetables so that it's vegetarian and inclusive. I've always wanted to try and quit meat, so this is the perfect chance. And maybe you could think of ideas for a nice little website, then enlist Mikasa and Elijah to help collect a heap of cast-offs from restaurants so we're recycling even more of the city's produce to keep the costs low?"

Smirking, Finn shook his head in pleasant disbelief. "You're a genius, Jasper. Truly. You've done most of the work already. Leave the rest to me."

NOW THAT dinner had fully settled and their business idea was safely in the pipeline, Finn was skimming one of Jasper's books in the lamplight since outside was shrouded in relative darkness.

"Jasper?" asked Finn, squinting to read the minuscule text. "What's an Oathstone?"

Jasper hadn't heard that word in many years. "It's something you can use to create an undying promise. If you swear on it, there's no going back, and if you somehow manage to break it or misplace it for good, your memory gets wiped."

"Interesting," Finn commented, scanning the words further. Jasper would give his left arm to be inside Finn's head for just a minute. "Your kind seems to enjoy wiping memories. Do these stones work on humans?"

"Yeah, actually. While mortals can't *do* magic, it still affects them. And there was a pretty big scandal when a woman got hold of one while drunk. Somehow managed to accidentally swear that she would never touch a drop of drink again. When she did the very next day, her entire memory was wiped, and she was committed to a clinic when the police found her aimlessly wandering around the city unable to recall her name."

"Wow," said Finn. "But how does anyone know what happened? I mean, if she didn't know what happened, how did anyone tell the tale?"

"Energy shift, remember? There's a lot of talented mage-sleuths in the city. I've often thought that must be a fun job."

Finn flipped a few more pages, then thumbed a new spot. "Look what it says here. 'In our world, subconscious manifestations are believed to be more dangerous than any spell that can be placed upon you by another mage.'"

Finn was gaping wide-eyed, but Jasper had drunk too many whiskeys and was failing to make the connection. "So? What good is that?"

"Well…." He let the book rest in his lap and turned to face him fully. "Recently, have you or have you not been feeling cooped up? Underappreciated? Isolated?"

"You know I have," he sighed. "But I'm still not following."

When Finn waved his hands about the air, the picture of exasperation, Jasper knew he was missing something. "That's why you're stuck here! Because you've been… stuck—" Finn tapped a finger on the side of his head "—in here."

The drunken veil lifted, and Jasper had a eureka moment. He felt like Thomas Edison, and he had Finn to thank.

"Oh shit!" he half laughed, half cried. "That makes perfect sense."

Finn winked. "Told you I could help."

Jasper shot up from the couch, unable to contain the energy coursing through him. He went straight to the door and swung it open, already seeing himself walk through and out to the world.

But when he ran at it, he bounced right back into the apartment.

When he heard Finn sniggering, Jasper moaned.

"But why?" He rubbed his head and gazed upward. "I thought…."

"Maybe…." Finn said behind him, getting up. "Maybe there's still some unresolved feelings. Give it time. This is a good thing. Now that we know what the problem is, we can work on fixing it."

Every fiber of Jasper's being was ready to protest, to come up with a multitude of reasons why he shouldn't have to wait because he'd waited long enough already. But Finn was right. He had to manage his expectations to see this through.

Even entertaining the idea of leaving the apartment after so long was exciting and scary.

Tomorrow, Jasper would make a conscious effort to sort his brain out. He would force himself to meditate for a full week if that's what it took to find inner peace, and he knew he would do it without a bite of food or drop of water if that's what it took to get out.

CHAPTER FIFTEEN

FINN WAS proud that they had made some progress with Jasper's situation, but when he found him lying on the couch the next day, the mage looked like he'd just finished watching the ten-hour version of Nyan Cat.

He'd seemed content last night… but he'd obviously reverted to old ways. Maybe Jasper thought that once Finn was in his life, busting out of the apartment was going to be a cakewalk. Maybe even instantaneous. But Finn had learned the hard way that life has a funny way of testing your limits. Clearly patience wasn't one of Jasper's strong suits, and it nagged at Finn that Jasper put so much stock in him when he was only human and Jasper was clearly something else.

"You all right?" Finn asked, glancing at the clock and seeing it read 6:45 a.m. Jasper was dressed in his grubby overalls, but his collection of paintbrushes lay resolutely in their pot. "Aren't you going to paint this morning? Finish off that weirdly flattering portrait of me?"

"Not yet, no." Jasper forced himself upright to make enough space for Finn to sit. "I just feel a bit dejected, you know? I was so hopeful to escape yesterday. I felt it in my bones. How dumb was I."

"Things will change," Finn assured. He offered a pat on the leg, then squeezed it so it didn't feel so platonic. "We'll get through this together."

"Easy for you to say." Jasper turned away to gaze out the window. "At least you get to go outside and go about the rest of your life."

"Like work my ass off?" Finn laughed. "It's manic at my office right now with everyone scrambling to find investors. Speaking of, I've got that stupid mixer later. Nobody understands the direction I want to keep us in, because it's not where the money's at. I swear to God, if that Purge day was a real thing...."

"Why not ditch?" Jasper suggested, whipping his head back around. There was a challenge in his eyes, and his tenacity was unexpected, but welcome. "Stay here with me instead. We can work on some more ideas for Scrumptious Sculptures."

Finn offered a small smile and wished it were as easy as that. But he was glad the mage was getting used to the idea of using his gift for something beyond sustenance. "Speaking of," Finn started, "do you want to rustle something up before I head off to the old grind? Or would you rather I go grab something for breakfast then pop back here?"

"No, no, I can do something," Jasper assured, irritation coating his tone as he got up and trotted to the kitchen. "I'll make the best damn eggs Benedict you've ever eaten. But the coffee here is garbage. Nothing like those fancy barista machines downtown. Would you mind?"

"Not at all." Finn wrapped his arms around Jasper in spite of the grubby apron. It was worth ruining a YSL cardigan just to hold himself in the moment with him.

Even if Jasper was feeling angsty, fed up, and generally over everything, his sulkiness was leagues better company than the false attitudes of anyone else Finn had ever been with. He grew happier in Jasper's presence, and they shared a soul-connecting moment when he leaned in for a kiss. It was slow and gentle, with unspoken layers in the simplest brush of lips.

Maintaining eye contact was important to remind Jasper he had Finn's full attention and would continue to for a long time to come. When the corners of his mouth lifted, the light returned to Jasper's eyes.

"Back in a tick." Finn grabbed his wallet off the table and left the door ajar as he dragged his heels from the apartment all the way down the stairs.

He was in dire need of caffeine, but the bigger concern was a hot shower and change of clothes. He'd have plenty of time to nip back to his place and get some coffee back to Jasper before the mixer.

The world was only just starting to wake up, and the trip across the street gave him a chance to ponder the dynamic between himself and Jasper.

There was an undeniable bond between them, but he wasn't sure if it was magnified simply because of the pressured situation Jasper was in... or the fact that Finn had never met anyone like Jasper before.

Finn simply prayed whatever they had between them lasted outside the walls of his apartment.

Back in his place, he noted how Jasper's was so small and cheap, and yet it had much more life in it than Finn's, which easily cost ten times more. The penthouse was in a near-constant spotless state, courtesy of the Roombas, self-cleaning appliances, and the weekly maid, but the sleek kitchen and open living area felt cramped and uninviting. He almost wished for Jasper's ghost to return so it wasn't so cold and lonely.

Finn showered on autopilot, pulled the tags off a new royal blue suit, slipped on some brown loafers, and went to grab decent coffee.

Now that people were rushing to work, Finn paid more attention. He wondered how many people of magical blood he'd come across in his life. Had he ever been made to do something against his will? He was shrewd enough to grasp that there wasn't much point dwelling on it. The past was in the past for a reason—it was unchangeable.

Still, it was interesting to speculate who might have abilities and what they might use them for in their everyday lives. He was fascinated to know who might be about to cause a scene or who was a charitable soul, ready to help out the vagrants littering the streets. He was willing to bet none of them would be half as humble with them as Jasper was. It was a testament to his innocence that he never bragged about his ability.

When Finn got back to Jasper's, the door was still ajar like he'd left it, but voices were coming from inside, and his heart skipped a few beats when he picked out a deep, masculine tone. Without thinking, his brain went straight to the worst possible outcome. The magical task force he had spoken about had found out about Finn's involvement, and they were probably minutes away from doling out unimaginable punishment. He had no idea who would be worse off.

But he couldn't be scared. Not now. Not after he and Jasper had clicked on a serious level. Taking a breath to steady himself, he barged in and brandished the hot coffee as a weapon.

But instead of powerful men in uniform, he found Jasper's friends sitting on the couch as he painted.

"Finn!" Jasper turned to him and shot an odd look when he saw coffees in his raised hands. "You remember Mikasa and Elijah, right?"

"Sure," said Finn, wondering how he could possibly have forgotten them. Mikasa's rich chocolate skin paired with a neon-yellow floral summer dress, and Elijah's ghost-pale twig-thin arms were on show courtesy of a polka dot tank top.

"Hiya!" Mikasa chirped, jumping up to come kiss Finn on the cheeks European-style. "Just gotta say, you and Jasper make the *cutest* couple ever!"

Finn arched an eyebrow and placed the coffees on the counter where Jasper's promised eggs Benedict was steaming away, looking effortlessly delectable. "I mean… we haven't actually asked each other… but thanks."

"Oops," she winked, taking a sip of his latte. "Delicious."

"Put that down, Mi-Mi," Elijah sighed, pushing her aside to shake hands. His voice was impressively deep, and Finn almost wanted to puff out his chest in front of Jasper.

When Mikasa put the drink down, she skipped back to the couch and watched Jasper decorate the nude painting of Finn as though she were having a private show.

Finn tried to roll with it and not feel self-conscious.

"Sorry," Elijah continued. "That woman has zero tact, and she's forever putting her foot in her mouth."

"I have ears, you know?" Mikasa giggled. "This apartment is the furthest thing from large."

"No worries." Finn was grateful he'd already taken a big swig on the way up. "It's no secret that me and Jasper are getting along great. And she's welcome to the drink."

"Aces," Mikasa called, raising both palms and spreading her fingers out ever so slightly to receive the coffee when it flew across the apartment to her.

"Whoa." Finn let his mouth fall open. Even though his stomach was growling, both Jasper and the eggs were forgotten.

"Cool, right?" Mikasa flashed her eyes at him over the rim of the paper cup. "If those eggs are going spare, I'll have those too?"

"Be my guest," Finn said, hunger abated.

Without a pinch of hesitation, Mikasa rested the cup between her thigh and the couch and created a table with her upturned hands. Finn watched in awe as the plate zipped across the room and settled into her grasp. She put it on her lap and didn't look up when she grabbed the cutlery.

"Show-off," Jasper snarked, claiming his own coffee and nodding his thanks. "Why couldn't I get a useful ability like that?"

Mikasa shrugged, busy with her meal. "It's so brave of Jas to tell you about our world. I wouldn't want to be the one on the end of that minefield."

"Brave or stupid," Elijah said. He punched Jasper on the arm and then stuffed his hands in his pockets. "I don't know how you're planning on keeping all this a secret. Someday someone at the Force is going to find out about this, and you'll get his memories wiped. Are you prepared for that, Mr. Anderson?"

When Finn understood that Elijah was talking to him, not Jasper, he soon felt everyone else's eyes on him too. Even Mikasa stopped chewing to hear his answer.

Who could ever be prepared for such a question?

Rather than make promises, Finn wanted to change topics. "That painting is coming along nice, Jasper."

Mikasa squealed. "Aw! Isn't he just the sweetest?"

"He is," Jasper agreed. "Not that being stuck here isn't a dream come true…. It would suck if I had to spend the rest of my days on a secluded island."

Elijah sighed in agreement. "I hear they have kickass beaches."

Since the spotlight was temporarily off Finn, he took a seat and pondered the weight of what Elijah had just said. It was no small thing to think about years' worth of memories being taken away at the click of someone's finger. Once again, Finn's feelings for Jasper were being tested so early on after their fateful meeting. He couldn't be certain whether it was a good thing that he didn't have an immediate answer.

"I want one." Mikasa continued to attack her food, totally oblivious to Finn's inner turmoil. "Where can I find myself a man who'll break the rules for me?"

"You'd have to actually go *look* for one if that's what you really want," Elijah said. "I can't imagine there's eligible bachelors lining up when you work in a canning factory."

"True," she agreed, "but the money's good."

Now that she was done with her food, the items clinked together as she made the plate and cutlery fly to the sink. Finn was almost certain that she only needed to use her eyes to perform the task—the flick of her wrist probably wasn't necessary. But these were hip New Yorkers to a T, and they did everything with a flourish.

"Oh," Finn said when the penny finally dropped. "You guys aren't together?"

"Hell no," Jasper said before his friends giggled in unison.

"Elijah is as gay as the day is long. He hasn't been with a girl in… what was it? Fourteen years?"

"Something like that," Elijah agreed, casting his eyes around the room. "Mi-Mi is New York's reigning hookup queen. Something about feminine expression." He shook his head fondly. "It's all very profound."

Finn couldn't help but go down the obvious road. As Elijah went to the windowsill and picked up one of Jasper's utterly lifeless potted plants, Finn wondered if he should consider him a threat. But that was just dumb old jealously talking.

He knew by now that *he* was Jasper's type, not this guy. Although he had very captivating and commanding eyes, Elijah looked like dining at Cheesecake Factory for a month would do him no harm.

"Well," Elijah started, "since Mikasa got to flaunt her stuff, maybe I should too."

Finn was more than ready to see more magic, and he actually leaned forward in his seat when Elijah placed Jasper's plant on the coffee table.

"You really should take better care of your plants, Jasper."

Jasper grunted in agreement as Elijah put his hands around the base of the potted plant and fixed his eyes on the blackened husk of whatever it had once been.

Finn couldn't believe his eyes as the leaves crackled and brightened back to a lively green. A fragrant lily scent laced the room as the plant continued to grow healthier and dominate his vision with the most vibrant colors. Within seconds, Elijah had reversed all traces of neglect, and the plant sitting in front of everyone filled Finn with both inspiration and optimism.

"Magic," Finn whispered, more to himself than anyone. "I just cannot get over it."

"Super cute," Mikasa said, eyeing Finn.

"It's called Biomancy," said Elijah.

"Like your Gastromancer?" Finn asked Jasper.

"Gastroman*cy*," he corrected. "I'm a Gastromancer, what I do is Gastromancy."

Shrugging with a smirk, Finn turned back to Elijah. Then he took a folding pen knife from his pocket, and Finn about shit his pants when the mage sliced open a thin line across his own forearm.

"Dude!" Finn shouted. "What are you doing?"

"No biggie." Elijah held out his wounded hand and wiggled his other one in front of it a few times. Before Finn's very eyes, the blood crawled back into the cut and Elijah's skin knit itself back up. "See? Good as new."

"This is lunacy," Finn said, grabbing Elijah's arm to stare at it. "So, like, can you even die?"

Elijah snorted. "Haven't exactly tried it. I do have to actually channel my energy to heal myself. So I probably can't if I get knocked unconscious."

"Wow." The possibilities of this guy's ability were mind-boggling. "Think of how useful you would be to modern science. If someone found out exactly what makes you tick, they could mimic the effects."

Elijah offered a weak smile. "Yeah, I don't really fancy being dissected on a lab bench somewhere in Area 51. There's enough suspicion surrounding that place as is."

"Plus," Mikasa put forth, "wouldn't it be just *bags* of fun to have over seven billion self-healing people walking around this planet? I mean… procreation doesn't seem to be slowing down anytime soon, so why not add potential immortality to the mix?"

"Less of all this big talk." Jasper wiped his apron and took a seat.

"But…," Finn struggled, mind still spinning, "don't you think it's a little selfish not to let the world know about you guys? Regardless of what you can do with your gifts?" He looked from each face crammed onto the ratty couch. But they were nonplussed, no doubt having already had this exact conversation a thousand times. "Think of what we could achieve on Earth if there were an institute for people with abilities like that."

"And think of how big the targets on our backs would be," said Mikasa. "Not to mention the whole societal imbalance it would create in the long run. Sure, it might be peachy for a while, but it would only be a matter of years before the uprisings and revolts would start."

When he snapped out of his postapocalyptic daydream, Finn realized where he was. "Right. I need to get to work."

"No!" cried Jasper and Mikasa in unison. Elijah snickered and put the plant back where he'd found it. It gave the room a lot more life, and Finn had a curious urge to see what wonders the man's apartment might hold.

"I have to." Finn shook his head. It was easy for these people to palm his job off as something trivial. "In the human world, these kinds of things matter."

Jasper put his paintbrush down and came to stroke his arm. "Sure… but… couldn't you stay a bit longer and just go into work later?"

Brow creased, Finn wondered how hard Gabriel would flip his lid if he asked to skip out on the mixer. Jasper was an important part of Finn's life now, and when you're getting to know someone in a romantic capacity, it's important to be willing to get to know their friends as well. Finn was having a good time seeing them demonstrate their abilities and getting to know their quirks. Even if they were totally batshit.

"Let me see what I can do," Finn said, taking his seat again as Mikasa clapped.

Finn whipped out his phone and texted as she and Elijah went to the kitchen to make tea. *Hey, Gabriel. I've got some things to take care of today, so I can't come in until later on this evening. I know you'll kill the mixer without me.*

A minute later, his phone buzzed with Gabriel's answer, the chime interrupting a pivotal part of Elijah's latest joke. *Not cool, man. The mixer is in just under an hour, and I'm totally fucking swamped over here. Your dad isn't going to like this one bit. Chances are, you'll be out on your ass by tomorrow morning.*

It took a lot of restraint for Finn to message back something amicable.

Fine. See you in ten.

Then he got up and crossed the room to wrap his arms around Jasper. "Gabe's not having any of it. I'm as good as fired if I don't go."

"Okay," Jasper said, turning to face Finn. "No worries. I'll see you later, though?"

"I can't promise anything," Finn said, feeling a knot in the pit of his stomach. He wanted to promise Jasper a lot more things than just another date. "I've got a lot on the agenda, but I'll try my hardest."

"Boring," Mikasa shouted, face scrunched up. "Aren't you, like, the CEO? Where's the fun in running a company if you can't work on your own schedule?"

"She has a point," Elijah said.

She *did* have a point, but Finn didn't need Elijah or anyone else to tell him as much. The annoying thing wasn't that she was outspoken… it was that he agreed with her and didn't know how to go about handling it.

Everything was so up in the air at the moment, and as much as he wanted to spend more time with Jasper and his friends, if he skipped out on the mixer, his career was well and truly done for. Deep inside, Finn's unwavering determination wouldn't let him back down just yet.

WALKING INTO the function room, Finn was surprised to see that Gabriel had sent out so many invitations and that so many had actually followed through on such short notice. But the room was brimming with people.

Dolled-up people, at that.

Clad in YSL blazers and Versace tuxedos with Cartier watches and Tiffany finery, they sipped flutes of prosecco and nibbled on French canapés. The air positively reeked of wealth, and as Finn took a moment to ground himself at the frankly tremendous head count, Gabriel was off like a flash, darting away from Finn to introduce himself to anyone who would make eye contact with him.

Throwing back his head, bellowing with laughter at a joke he'd probably already missed the punchline to, Gabe wasted no time putting on a charming façade that Finn had never seen at work—all to promote the company.

After the slow decline and eventual collapse of their print magazine, it was actually refreshing to see company branding outside the office walls. As well as an idle on-screen demo of the app, there were Zest banners and Zest table runners to support Zest-sourced refreshments. There was even lemon-shaped bunting strung across the ceiling, for crying out loud.

Clearly his father had spared no expense on his latest ploy, and Finn was only slightly disappointed that the man of the hour wasn't there to see it all in person. And coupled with Gabriel's subterfuge, the fun of representing a company built from the ground up was gone.

"Thank you for coming," Finn said in passing to a group of men, some of whom were busy scrolling through their cell phones while others chattered and let the smoke of their cigars foul the air.

Since when was that suddenly not illegal?

Next was a gaggle of women dressed in feathered petticoats and crisp updos. Blinking slowly, thanking them for their time, Finn wondered if there was a Victorian dress code. He felt like he was in a goddamn episode of *Poirot*.

"Honestly, Robert…." Gabriel's voice had somehow dropped two octaves as he launched straight into the sales pitch, and Finn could swear he was standing on the balls of his feet to match the height of the city's mayor. "I have full faith in our latest plan, and I am confident that *Zest* will have positive equity in no less than five years from initial investment."

Dragging his feet, Finn tipped his head to a few more people and then grabbed a drink and lingered at the back wondering exactly how long he could get away with pretending to have his head stuck in his cell phone. There were only so many emails to look at and tiresome business notes to reread. Maybe he could sneak to the bathroom. Gabriel was doing a much better job at faking it, anyway. But then, it probably wasn't fake. Where Finn was already bored to tears, Gabriel seemed genuinely interested in this kind of environment.

If his dad were here, he'd no doubt be disappointed in Finn's lack of interest. But as much as he wanted to prove himself to his parents and keep his monthly allowance, his heart wasn't in it. Jasper had opened Finn's eyes to a new way of thinking. How much more rewarding was it for everyone involved if you stopped caring about profit margins and sales ploys. Finn wanted the food and the artistry that went into creating it to speak for itself.

"Finley Anderson!" Somebody called, pulling Finn out of his self-induced reverie. *Oh Jesus.* He hadn't heard anyone call him by that name in over five years. Even his father had stopped when Finn threatened to leak their sales statistics.

The man walking toward him was none other than Oliver Trigwell, the red-faced former director of Traffix Brokers—a subsidiary of a leading New York trader. It was public knowledge that the man with the full-on Santa Claus beard was desperate to come out of retirement and get back in the game—any game. Problem was, there wasn't a brokerage in the country who would offer him a position ever since he lost a total of $320 million after investing in fidget spinner knockoffs that never took off. Also, though he had friends in high places, Finn had heard rumors they wouldn't help him.

Shaking the man's callused hand with a pasted-on smile, Finn knew exactly how the exchange would pan out. It would start with jovial small talk, Oliver perhaps even throwing out a compliment or two, either about his hair or how he totally didn't disapprove of Finn's *eclectic* lifestyle. Then things would get serious and talk would turn to Finn's father and how Oliver just so happened to have the funds to save the frankly tanking company.

"A fine turnout, my boy," Oliver boomed. "And you're looking sharp too! Is that a new suit?"

Aaaand there it was.

"Yes," Finn said, not bothering to elaborate. Maybe that would give him the hint.

"Say, Finley," he continued, pounding Finn on the arm. "One of my wife's nephews also enjoys the company of men. The kid's name is Thomas Larkin—perhaps you know him?"

Sniggering, Finn sipped his drink. "No. We don't all have each other on speed dial, Mr. Trigwell."

"Right. Yes, of course." The pot-bellied man eyed the room carefully, letting the weight of the awkward moment sit on Finn's chest. "Well, would you take a look at all these wannabe investors. I'm impressed this many people are interested in putting their coin behind a mobile game."

"It's an app," Finn corrected. "And the future is forward."

Closing his eyes, Finn mentally pinched himself for reciting his father's cringeworthy motto.

Though Oliver himself was broke, he had plenty of friends who weren't. If Finn's head were more in the game, this would be the point where he could launch into a spiel about how much net growth the company would have in the next quarter alone, how beneficial their way of thinking was for the social economy, not to mention the positive effect on locally grown and sourced food.

And yet, Finn's lips remained sealed.

He missed Jasper like mad. If he were at Finn's side, he would have no problem shutting down the bigoted man with a witty remark. Laugh it all off and move on to the next investor who actually had the funds. Then again, if the mages were out and proud in the public eye, things would be unequivocally better for countless reasons—efficiency, pleasure, sustainability. It was almost dangerous to think about just how much money that little recycling trick could save his company.

Suddenly, Finn felt a physical tug to see Jasper's face and run his hands through his soft golden hair. See how slowly he could undo his zipper…

"Whatever you say," Oliver continued, apparently still intent on trying to garner Finn's rapidly diminishing attention. "I swear, if this is all the twenty-first century has to offer, we're all in big trouble."

"Then why are you here?" Finn asked, patience finally melted onto the carpet. "Do you have any interest in the food industry at all?"

Arching an eyebrow, Oliver chortled instead of taking offense. "Look at my gut, dear boy. This thing didn't come from anything but a love of food, now, did it?"

Finn tried not to roll his eyes too hard as he went back to his cell, more to catch a break than to pay attention to the notification that had pinged through, which was a text from Gabriel across the room.

Between the smug bastard flaunting company statistics like they were Olympic awards, he had found time to text Finn and tell him to play nice.

Well, screw that. Gabriel wouldn't know the first thing about running an environmentally sustainable company if the very idea decided to grow a body and sock him in the face. Profit was the man-child's sole concern, and the idiot had tunnel vision. He'd sooner push organic farmers aside and dissolve every last small business in the city if it meant he would secure his place at the top with the big boys. Those weren't the ethics of a company Finn had much faith in.

Oliver cleared his throat, begging for yet more attention and refusing to let the conversation die. "Just how much would a 1 percent share cost, kid?"

"I can't remember," Finn dismissed. The exact figure had come to mind instantly, but he was trying very hard to bite his tongue and keep his real thoughts to himself. "Please excuse me."

"But—"

Leaving Oliver disgruntled in half speech, Finn wove through the bodies stacking up by the free food.

Gabriel had managed to insert himself into yet another group, this one primarily consisting of older gentlemen with goatees.

When he didn't immediately notice him, Finn took a leaf out of Oliver's book and cleared his throat. "Let's do this, Gabe."

Narrowing his eyes, Gabriel lifted his glass in some kind of salute. "Gentlemen, it was a pleasure. I'll make sure to catch up with you later on."

Finn heard Gabriel snorting in disgust.

"You're a mess, Finny." He made sure to keep his voice to a whisper as he took a few more strides to reach Finn's side. "Have you made even one attempt to garner anyone's interest? Having a lengthy powwow with Oliver Trigwell doesn't count."

Eyeing him lazily, Finn drank in notes of genuine contempt as Gabriel tapped a few commands on his tablet.

"I think you need to chill out a bit," Finn suggested.

"Ladies and gentlemen," Gabriel called out, doing precisely the opposite. When his voice didn't quite settle the crowd, he found a spoon to tap on the side of a flute. "Please grant me your attention for a few moments. Thank you kindly."

Turning around, Finn assessed the crowd's mood. It seemed to be an amusing mix of contentment, forced enthusiasm, and half-drunken courtesy.

"For anybody who has been living under a rock for the last century," Gabriel continued, forcing a chuckle, "we have prepared an app demonstration for *Zest*."

Staring into space, Finn wondered exactly how Gabriel was going to claim credit on the demo when it was Finn who had pushed his team for two straight days to get it together. He explicitly recalled Gabriel taking more interest in extended lunches with Madison than doing grunt work.

"Now," the distant voice began, "if he can stop daydreaming about rainbows, my assistant here will demo the app of the hour."

Assistant? He threw a scowl at Gabriel. Was he fucking serious?

Joining the rumbling crowd, Gabriel laughed the moment off, nodding his head toward the screen with a look saying *hurry up.*

Frowning, with heat creeping up his neck, Finn plugged in the iPad and initiated the sequence. After swiping through the Welcome screen and hearing the room reverberate the cute citrus-burst jingle, he glided through to the New User interface. It was supposed to pop up with a handy login menu where you could tap any of your favorite social medias for quick access, but it took Finn all of two seconds to realize the epilepsy-inducing flickering menu wasn't working as it should, and everyone else in the room had been quick to notice.

"What's going on, man?" Gabriel asked, voice returning back to his usual whining pitch, leaning over to tap at the screen.

"I don't know," Finn admitted, though he knew Gabriel repeatedly tapping the admin overlay was doing the opposite of good. "It was optimized just fine last night. It's probably just a simple bug. Gimme a sec."

This was no time to panic, but the crease on Finn's brow deepened as he furiously typed in some code. As he was doing so, Gabriel tried to settle the crowd by telling some kind of joke—no doubt at Finn's expense.

"Nearly there," Finn whispered, more to himself than anyone else. He was happy to have found that the issue was a pesky little virus that the tablet wasn't equipped to handle, but it took another full minute to use another piece of software to purge the residual cache and get things back to normal.

"Here we go." Finn said indicating to Gabriel he was ready to continue. It was more than odd. The device hadn't shown the first sign of these issues last night. So where the hell had they come from?

Clapping his hands together once, summoning the audience's attention back from the hushed conversations that had broken out, Gabriel returned to his business voice. "Now that our master solutionizer has fixed the issue, it's time for take two!"

"Apologies," Finn half muttered as he addressed the crowd. "Now if you see here, when you try to log in for the first time, you can simply—"

A few members of the crowd gasped while others snickered. Turning back to the screen, Finn saw that, instead of showing them how to log in to the app they were supposed to be investing in, he'd brought up his own email and all of the incredibly sensitive, incredibly personal data within.

"Jesus Christ," Gabriel said, putting down his drink so he could pinch the bridge of his nose. "Just… step aside."

"No," Finn insisted. "No. I can fix this. I can."

Panic started to freeze the blood in his veins. How had he missed this when testing his team's solution?

Finn flinched as Gabriel wrenched his hands off the tablet and shoved him aside with his hips.

"Why don't you just head back to the office?" Gabriel suggested, voice dripping with scorn. "Catch up on something simple like inventory reports. Oh, and maybe try not to trip over any cables and set fire to anything on your way out."

Nodding his head, it took a huge amount of willpower for Finn to admit defeat. There was nothing left to say. He should've just stayed back at Jasper's place with his friends.

Turning around, he tried not to acknowledge everyone openly gazing at him as he strode out of the room. Dazed as he was, Gabriel had probably been right to take over, because Finn had been distracted for the whole function and he knew precisely why. Not only had he forced himself to participate in an event he was no longer enthusiastic about, but Jasper was almost always on the forefront of his brain.

Shutting the door, Finn didn't fully register Gabriel's words until he started walking out of the foyer and they began to echo in his head. "Ah, and here is Madison with the backup device," he'd said. "This one will work fine. Now. As you can see ladies and gentlemen…."

So. Gabriel had sabotaged him in front of everyone just so he could bitch about it later and try to get him fired. *Fantastic.*

Out on the street, Finn's consciousness lost its only reason to remain in work mode. Letting himself drift on a sea of Jasper-related thoughts, there was a list of problems he needed to solve.

First and foremost—how was he going to get his mage out of that apartment?

CHAPTER SIXTEEN

IN THE wake of Mikasa and Elijah's exit, it didn't take long for Jasper to get bored.

He didn't want to be separated from Finn for any longer than necessary, and it was a good idea to carry on practicing his projections anyway. But Jasper had no idea where he worked, or how long he would be at the mixer.

Meh. If he was still at the event, Jasper would simply come back to his body.

With fingers crossed, he sat on the floor and closed his eyes. It seemed to help his projections when Finn was close in proximity, but this time, all Jasper could think to do was focus on him. He pictured his angled face, the sandalwood scent always clinging around his day-old stubble, and his kind energy and the warm smile that went with it. Surely that was enough of a connection to transport him to wherever Finn was?

Sure enough, when Jasper opened his eyes, he was in a cute little office lined with Warhols. Very impressive. This office no doubt belonged to Finn. But he wasn't alone.

"What do you think you're playing at?" the new guy asked, both hands spread out on Finn's desk as he leaned down to intimidate. Was this Gabe? The one Finn had been curt on the phone to a few days ago?

The guy was muscle-set with a jawline to die for, and his gray tux offset his blond surfer curls. It looked like he belonged on the white-sand beaches of Cali, not holed up in a New York office with Jasper's man. Evidently, this was a bad time for an intrusion.

"I know you set me up earlier," said Finn. "It's a shame, really. If you were any good at your job, you wouldn't have to stoop so low."

Upon arrival, Jasper had intended to do a striptease to the imaginary beat of a Christina Aguilera hit. But he had second thoughts after sensing the aura in the room.

Finn was stressed out. Whether it was from the mixer or not didn't much matter. He might as well have had *I need emotional support* tattooed on his forehead, and when Finn caught sight of what was happening in front of him, his mouth popped open.

Smiling, Jasper was glad Gabriel was too busy outlining all the reasons why Finn had been acting weird at the mixer. Floating across the room, Jasper looked out at New York from a massive expanse of window. This vantage was leagues better than the one in his apartment. He could paint so many people from this view.

"I think you've made your point," Finn said to Gabriel. Clearly, he wanted to get the man out of the way ASAP. "Why don't we go over the final figures at the end of the day?"

"The sooner we consolidate our information the better," said Gabriel. Impatience dripped from his tone, and Jasper wondered if this was how he usually spoke. "This place will have people begging us to sponsor them within a month. But I don't imagine you'll be around much longer to see that happen. When did you become so lazy, Finn?"

"Because...." Finn struggled to answer. "Surely you—uhh... jotted down some names for investors? I would've thought dealing with that takes priority?"

"Hmph," Gabriel muttered. "I guess you're right. Maybe all of this chatter your father's been prattling on about is finally sinking in. Good to know."

When footsteps scraped along the carpet and the door clicked open and then clicked closed, Finn sighed.

"What the fuck, Jasper!"

"Hi," he said meekly, turning around to see deep lines on Finn's face.

"How did he not see you? Are you harnessing more power or something?"

"Pfft," said Jasper. "As if."

Though he enjoyed the idea, he knew it was extremely unlikely. The only way to gain extra power was through a bequeathing ritual that had lethal consequences if not done properly—something Jasper had neither the money nor associates for, not to mention nerve. And yet, even if his gastronomy gift wasn't about to change, who's to say his progress with projections wasn't a sign things were on the uptick?

For the first time in a long while, a foreign feeling began to tickle Jasper. Hope. It was a nice feeling to have. But Finn didn't look like he had much of that at the moment.

Touching down on the springy carpet, Jasper padded over to him. "Are you okay?"

"Yeah, fine." After absently scratching the back of his neck, Finn made a move to get up.

"No, stay there." Softly, Jasper planted his hands on Finn's shoulders. It was a strange sensation—squishier than flesh ought to be, but still firm enough to detect edges. "Had a rough day, I take it? That Gabe guy seems like a dick."

"Hah," said Finn. "That's too kind a word. I swear he set me up to fail today. It was beyond humiliating."

"Aw, babe," Jasper said and instantly cringed at himself. As he worked the muscles in Finn's shoulders, he found it exceptionally curious how objects would only react to his touch if he wanted them to. He was still a novice at all this astral-projection stuff, and it was taking a while for him to get used to the semisolid feel of his own limbs.

"I think I'm in the wrong trade," Finn said. "Whenever I'm in this office, all I seem to do is get angry."

"I'd have to agree." Jasper stopped massaging him so that he could park his butt on the desk and get a proper look at Finn. "This place is too clinical for you. You need a space where you can really pursue your creativity. Which is why our joint project is looking less like a pipe dream and more like divine intervention."

"Yeah," Finn agreed, filled with new-found enthusiasm. "Enough of this defeatist crap. It's pointless. I'll make our venture work if it's the last thing I do."

"That's the spirit!" Jasper beamed as he extended an index finger to trace the lines of Finn's jaw. "We can do anything we want if we put our minds to it."

"Are you thinking what I'm thinking?" Finn's tone of voice had dipped dramatically, and when he grazed his teeth on his bottom lip, Jasper figured it was the first time in his life he could read minds. "If you can touch my face, you can touch other things…."

Jasper hopped down from the desk, eager to return to his original intent. He'd planned on the striptease just for fun, but if he actually got to touch Finn, so much the better.

The moment Jasper reached for Finn's zipper, his knees buckled of their own accord. Surprised, he held his hands aloft and saw them growing more translucent. Of course there was a limit to his projections. Whether it was a time restriction or something energy based, did it have to be right now?

How freaking typical.

"So," Jasper started, perplexed to also find himself short of breath, "it seems we can't really do *anything* we want…."

As his form began to flicker, he peered up at Finn. Before he was transported back to his body, Jasper caught the beginnings of Finn's smile and his eyes rolling all the way to the ceiling.

CHAPTER SEVENTEEN

IN JUST a week of knowing Jasper, Finn savored their routine. Normally he hated sharing his space with anyone—let alone in a bed a whole two feet smaller than the king in his penthouse. But being shacked up with Jasper was different. *He* was different. To anyone he'd ever met. He knew when to spoon and when to keep his distance, and even though he snored like a thoroughbred horse dreaming of an earthquake… it was unbelievably endearing.

After some terse negotiations, Gabriel saw the merit of letting Finn work opposite shifts to him. They were butting heads too often, and it was affecting staff morale as well as draining Finn's mental stamina. Finn knew he would have more energy to work during the night if it meant the asshat wasn't around to breathe down his neck.

Jasper spent his time either painting or drumming up more names for his edible sculptures, and Finn was proud that his latest form of expression was something that could be so easily marketed. People would go nuts for this level of creativity, especially when it also happened to taste so heavenly.

Whenever they took a break, they either delved into more mage literature to research Jasper's predicament or made out on the couch. Finn didn't feel guilty for falling on the latter most of the time.

Jasper had been filled with a restless energy over the last few nights. Sex may have helped… and Finn was ever conscious that they hadn't yet gone the full length… but after working twice as hard at his job, he'd been too tired to have the type of sex he wanted to have with Jasper.

On one particularly horny night, Jasper had woken Finn up and coaxed him into a mutually beneficial oral exchange. It was amazing to be so comfortable and intimate with someone as sexy as Jasper, but when they had full-on sex, Finn wanted it to be special, one of a kind, just like the mage who blew his mind on a daily basis.

But it was a different kind of experience altogether to wake up and see the light streaming in on Jasper's cute face, golden hair fanned across the pillow whenever it wasn't tucked up in that bun. Finn wanted to lie in and maybe even request a special breakfast. But he had to get to work. Just because Gabriel wasn't there to breathe down his neck in person, he had no qualms about pinging over fifty emails a day.

Finn put on the old clothes he had with him, and though he was keen to return home and swap into a fresh outfit, it was a nice change of pace to not be so uptight around someone so handsome.

"Hey, you," he said, leaning in for a hug when Jasper turned around.

When Jasper squealed, Finn thought it was from surprise. But when he pulled away and Jasper stared at his chest, he realized that he'd gotten a fresh splodge of phthalo blue on his blazer.

"Fuck my life," Finn sighed, stripping. "We're definitely going to have to get me some spare clothes round here."

"Yeah," Jasper agreed. It was the little things that solidified their togetherness. "That or I'll just have to match you and spend my days painting naked."

"I wouldn't say no to that," Finn admitted. "How's it coming along, by the way?"

It was still a bit weird that Jasper had been painting him all this time, especially while he'd had his friends over for dinner, but now that Finn knew Jasper, he was more flattered than creeped out to be a part of the raunchy soap opera.

"I'm pretty much done." Jasper pulled away the tarp and unveiled the painting. "Just need to wait a couple weeks for it to dry so I can varnish it and add it to the collection. Yours will be pride of place, of course."

"Amazing," Finn remarked. The pose Jasper had caught him in on the elliptical was stunning, and the member dangling between the bars was modest, to say the least. Just looking at it knowing Jasper had spent hours thinking about how to perfectly capture Finn's physique made him all tingly. "I think there's a slight error with the composition. Just… there…."

"There is?" Jasper leaned in close, a crease forming on his brow. "I thought I'd gotten it just right."

"Perhaps you ought to take another look in person?" Finn asked. "So that you might compare the two?"

When he caught the meaning, Jasper drew himself back up to full height and sniggered. "The painting is fine, isn't it?"

"It's perfect," Finn said. "Just like that sweet ass of yours."

"Smooth." Jasper leaned in for a kiss. "Someone's horny this morning, eh? I think I'd like to wait for when the time is right, you know? You've got so much going on at work right now, and I know all of this is a mindfuck."

Jasper waved his hands around his body to indicate he meant himself. And he was right—each new day was another mindfuck. And Jasper was also right that they should wait to have proper sex when the time presented itself. Finn was planning on being with Jasper for the long haul, and he was confident the expert painter was used to the notion that there was no sense rushing perfection.

FINN COULDN'T remember the last time he'd had such a relaxing afternoon.

Watching Jasper practice his edible creations proved to be a delightful form of entertainment, and after Finn had pilfered the phone numbers of Jasper's friends and messaged them about bakery business, they took regular breaks to snuggle on the couch and make out.

Just as he was about to deepen their latest kiss, Finn's phone buzzed.

Ignoring it, he tried to recenter himself in the moment. When another two texts chimed, Finn was about to toss his phone to the side when Gabriel drop-called him.

Huffing—he really wasn't interested in anything the man had to say—but things were so tense at the moment, it would be to Finn's detriment if he let it slide. He glanced at the little preview box and was surprised the biometric mechanic worked after he'd wrinkled his face so much.

"That's odd."

"What's up?" Jasper asked. "Not a booty call from another lover, I hope?"

"Nah, silly. Just some messages from Gabe. Says he wants to meet."

"Right now?" It was Jasper's turn to scrunch up his face. "Aren't you two supposed to be avoiding each other or something?"

"Yeah," Finn agreed. "But he thinks he's got a wealthy investor on the hook, and it's apparently time sensitive."

"And he can't sort that out on his own?" Jasper stroked Finn's thigh with undeniable purpose. "We've never gone past this stage."

Sighing, Finn met Jasper's longing gaze. "I know. It's not my idea of fun, trust me. But it's weird, even for him, to hound me like this. It must be important. He'll only give me grief for it tomorrow if I don't go see what's going on. I'll make it up to you. I promise."

"Okay, okay," said Jasper. "While you're gone, I'll think of some remuneration methods. Hurry back," he added when Finn kissed his cheek and rose to his feet. "I'll keep the door on the latch and have dinner waiting for us."

"I look forward to it." Finn captured a mental image of Jasper gazing up at him with his big blue eyes, looking all kinds of sexy, and then he left the apartment.

It would do well to keep him in mind when he dealt with whatever bullshit Gabriel had in store.

THE ADDRESS Gabriel sent was for the Four Seasons downtown. So, this new client was wealthy, indeed. In lieu of all the workouts he'd foregone, he wanted to stretch his legs, but the rapidly darkening skies had brought on a bitter cold, and he wasn't about to waste forty minutes walking.

The sooner he got back to furthering that moment with Jasper, the better. His lust was sharper than a knife.

When the Uber pulled up, Finn threw himself in the back and scrolled through some notes to brush up on the latest statistics forecast. Whoever he'd be meeting would want to know the profit margins for at least the next five years, and Finn did some quick math to figure out how much he could embellish without completely stretching the truth.

Since the driver made good time, Finn pinged her a respectable tip and said his thanks. Then he climbed out and hugged his coat. There were a bunch of people braving the streets despite the temperature, and he had to slalom between three separate droves of selfie-happy tourists to gain access to the steps.

He walked through the revolving door and quickly located a largely 1920s-themed semicircular bar, where a Debussy concerto filtered over the hushed tones of elegant people deep in conversation. On first glance, Finn wasn't able to spot his colleague. It was unlikely that Gabriel was running late since this investment opportunity was apparently a time-sensitive thing. As Finn weaved through the throngs, he also couldn't see any of his normal clientele. There were a few men on their own here and there, but they were absorbed in either cell phones or overpriced cocktails.

"Tom Collins," Finn stated once he'd sunk himself into a raised armchair around the bar. "Extra sugar."

When the bartender nodded curtly and turned his attention to the spirits rack, Finn reached for his phone and thumbed a text.

Thanks for ditching me, douchebag. I came all this way and you're not even here? Who's this big bad guy you've pussied out on?

Ever the tormentor, Gabriel took a full two minutes to reply.

The fuck, man? I'm busy at the gym. Thought you could handle something like that on your own?

Positively livid, Finn shoved the phone back in his pocket and chucked a twenty at the bartender. Then he downed half his drink. He was grateful the swanky bar had imported London gin, as he preferred the more prominent juniper berry taste. Still, the particularly dry sting didn't do enough to lessen his anger. He slid off the chair, drained the glass, and was about to head on back to Jasper's when somebody spoke.

"You really shouldn't hold it against Mr. Fernandez," came a sharp feminine voice to his immediate left. "He's got a weak mind, and it makes him very easy to bend to my will."

When he turned, Finn was glad the bartender wasn't in range for his literal spit-take. The woman he now gawped at had sleek French tips wrapped around the stem of a martini glass, a familiar razor-sharp bob that gave symmetry to her petite shoulders, and a golden braid around her collar, which hung just above a boldly plunging neckline.

Well, shit. Jasper's mom was also wearing a devious little smile, and Finn didn't have the first idea what it—or she—was doing there.

CHAPTER EIGHTEEN

WITH A glass of rosé at his side, Jasper sat at the window, watching New York's late-night pantomime unfold. It had been almost an hour since Finn left, and there was no telling what he and his coworker were up to.

His scorching hot coworker, mind.

To remind himself that Finn's absence was totally fine, Jasper puttered about the apartment, creating jobs for himself. His shabby bookcase was crying out for a dusting, and that kitchen sink was in desperate need of bleaching—not to mention the labyrinth of coaster marks on the coffee table. How had they escaped his notice for so long?

He had to chill out and take a breather. So what if Finn was spending time out-of-hours with a Chris Hemsworth lookalike? It meant nothing. Doubtless he had been tempted in the past... but that was the in the past, right? There was zero sexual chemistry when Jasper dropped in on their heated conversation after the mixer—only anger.

Though he'd tried it once and despised it, Jasper wished he had a pack of Marlboro Reds to settle his nerves like they did in old Hollywood films. Maybe Elijah had something to take the edge off—something natural, of course. The dude had an affinity for plants, after all.

Once the sink and draining board were clean enough to eat a five-course meal from, the cobwebs in the top corners of the ceiling began to glint like spun silver. It was like a veil had been lifted and every speck of dirt had become the true culprit of the mage's snare. All of it had to be purged.

The more he cleaned, the easier his brain seemed able to settle on the negatives. Once again, he'd been too hopeful. He had allowed himself to believe that things were about to change, that destiny had intervened and brought Finn along as a knight in tuxedo-shaped armor. Maybe he'd been wrong about him. Maybe the pair weren't thrown together by fate.

Or, more likely, maybe Jasper had simply drunk too much and he should get his priorities straight. A bit of jealousy simply meant he cared. And anyway, Finn's heart was in the right place. It wasn't his fault things weren't going according to Jasper's rudderless plan.

He would get out eventually. It was only a matter of time.

Next he ran to get a step ladder and feather dusters from the closet. If he kept up this level of self-induced OCD, he ran a very real risk of a psychotic break.

He tried an assortment of chores and finally settled on painting— anything to keep his mind occupied and away from the temptation to project to Finn and see what he was really up to. To do so would break their trust, and without a healthy mindset, Jasper knew he didn't stand much of a chance at true happiness.

CHAPTER NINETEEN

THE WAY Jasper's mom held Finn's gaze made his palms sweat. Back in Jasper's hallway, she had been a crude version of the Wicked Witch of the West. Now, as Finn paid for another drink in advance—tipping heavily to atone for his uncouthness—she acted like butter wouldn't melt in her mouth, and her saccharine smile set his teeth on edge.

"Finley," she said, holding out a limp hand. "What a pleasure it is to see you again."

When he finally returned to earth, Finn was cordial enough to squeeze her hand gently but hardly about to kiss it. "Evangeline. Seeing you here is a small surprise, you'll grant."

"Call me Eva," she said, winking an expertly smoke-shadowed lid.

Pulling up his stool again, Finn cut the shit and leveled with her. "I'm going to go ahead and assume you aren't in the market for culinary investments. How did you get Gabriel to contact me?"

"How do you think?" She took a sip of her drink and toyed with the toothpick-skewered olive. "It took all of two minutes to find where you worked. Even less than that for me to speak to that cofounder of yours. As I said before… terribly weak-willed, that one."

Grinning, Finn took a certain amount of pleasure in that. He wondered whether he could be so easily manipulated by her gift. He also wondered what his staff made of the daunting woman waltzing her way up to his floor without a visitor's lanyard.

"What do you want?" Finn asked. "Not to be rude, but this is all a bit cloak-and-dagger, and I don't have the patience for mysteries."

"I'd like to know your intentions with my son."

Finn openly guffawed. "That's all this is? An intervention from a dutiful parent?"

"Don't laugh at me," Eva said, voice calm. "When you have kids of your own, you might understand the lengths parents go to."

"I like Jasper," Finn assured. Was that what she needed to hear? A candid expression of his feelings? "I like him a lot, in fact."

"Regardless," she dismissed, waving a hand, "this is no joke. I fear your involvement will make things worse for him, not better. What's happening to him is a very personal test, and you're only serving to complicate things."

"Everything will work out just fine," Finn defended. "It has to. I've been thinking about organizing an art exhibition to showcase his talents for when he gets out."

"Oh?" The increase in her vocal octaves suggested genuine surprise. "And how do you propose to keep this up even if he does acquire freedom? You two are from different worlds. This little fling you've got going? It might seem long-term… but it can't last. Call it destiny, call it what you want. The mixing of blood is all the same to MRF—they don't look on it kindly."

Finn took a minute to consider her words. It wasn't anything he hadn't thought of before. He and Jasper had touched on the Magical Regulation Force just the other day. And yet it was still painful to hear her verbalize the inevitability of their separation.

Finn was ready to fight for whatever it was they had blossoming. "I've been reading up on Oathsto—"

"Heavens, shut up," Eva snapped, eyes darting across the bar.

For just a moment, she looked shocked, as if she'd put bare hands in an unprotected breaker box. Just as suddenly, she appeared to be the picture of serenity.

With her eyes closed, Eva did some deep breathing. She looked like she belonged on a yoga mat in the mountains of Indonesia while she aligned her chakras. Finn was wondering how long the melodramatics were going to take when, before he could make sense of it, the chattering of the other people in the room silenced. When he turned around, he saw them rise in unison, with blank yet content expressions on their faces as they shuffled like placid zombies toward the exit.

The bartender was also making an unhurried exit, but when Eva opened her eyes again, she clicked her fingers at him. "Leave the bottle."

Obediently complying without a word of protest, he placed the gin on the antislip mat and continued his involuntary journey.

Once she poured herself a generous measure and fetched herself a fresh olive, Eva side-eyed Finn. "You shouldn't speak of such things in public.

"Evidently."

Clearing a room of people with nothing but your mind was impressive, absolutely, but Finn wasn't sure what to make of the blatant display. How was it acceptable for this woman to lecture him on the risks of exposing their world when she'd just flaunted exactly that herself? Wouldn't her activity get flagged by the MRF?

Finn decided to bite his tongue. Jasper did say she knew how to fly under the radar, and the mother of his would-be boyfriend probably wouldn't appreciate being labeled a hypocrite.

"Since Jasper is the reason you even know about their existence," she started, spearing another olive, "I have no doubt the boy failed to mention that Oathstones are a terribly tricky thing." If it was a question, Eva didn't bother waiting for a response. "The smallest hiccup in the vow you make can cause drastic results. You have to be extremely specific with the wording, lest it uphold something entirely different from your original intent."

Finn nodded. "Have you made a vow before?"

"No, but I know plenty who have. A friend of mine... well, to cut a long story short, where she set out to shield the behavior of her geriatric father from MRF, she slipped up one word and now has to spend every Tuesday on her hands and knees scrubbing the toilets of a Fortune 500 company until they go bankrupt. Which isn't likely to happen for the next, I don't know, thousand years."

Finn tried to imagine the original wording versus the jacked-up one, but he just couldn't see it.

"Can you wish for anything you like?" he wondered.

"They aren't for wishing," she informed, sternly. "The stones are born from trust, and they exist to further bonds by making an everlasting promise to another person."

"Interesting," Finn mused. If he could somehow source one, maybe there was hope for himself and Jasper after all. Things didn't have to look gloomy and bleak so long as he remained positive. "How can I get my hands on one?"

"Are you joking?" Eva giggled. It was the first time Finn had heard her express any form of pleasure, and the dainty trill as she tipped back her head suited her better than the earlier façade. "Never before has a human laid a hand on artifacts from Orthos."

"Why should that matter?" Finn squinted, not caring who or what Orthos was. "Who's to say it's not good to break the mold and do something new?"

She cocked an eyebrow and stared at him squarely. "You are aware that to break the vow is to have your memory wiped—completely and utterly." When Finn nodded, her eyebrow shot even higher. "Tell me," she said. "What would you even do with one?"

"Find a way to make a life with your son," said Finn. "All I want to do is make him happy."

Eva's breath hitched and she narrowed her eyes and fell silent. Another first. He watched the cogs turn in her brain as she dug through her purse, and he got the impression the lady wasn't often lost for words.

"Gah, where is it?" she muttered to herself, squinting at the leather lining. "Oh, there you are."

There was a measured look on Eva's face as she held aloft a black business card lettered with a bright red serif font. Slowly and almost warily, she placed it on the counter and intently watched Finn's reaction as he studied it.

"Blayze Martinez?" he read out loud and wondered why he was being presented with an Etsy card for somebody who made handmade trinkets. He picked up the weighted sheet and flipped it over. Showcased on the back was a miniaturized collection of decorative glassware pieces, and even though the artistry was both evident and impressive,

Finn was clueless as to their relevance. "Are you suggesting I buy one of these for Jasper? Is that how I'm supposed to seal our bond?"

Eva rolled her eyes and smiled with something closely resembling pity. "If you're serious about being with my son in this capacity, then you're serious about acquiring an Oathstone. This guy right here is the one to talk to. He can be a difficult son of a bitch at the best of times, and getting him to part with one of these ancient relics is no small task to begin with. But, as the Fate's will it, he's also Jasper's ex, so your task will doubtless be that much harder."

Finn didn't much like the sound of anything he'd just heard, and he screwed up his face, but as she got up from her stool and slung her bag around her shoulder, Eva didn't seem interested in waiting around to hear his response.

"You can either rise to this momentous occasion or fall flat on your face." She turned around and slinked toward the exit, casually waving a hand behind her. "The choice is yours."

THE LOCATION on the business card read like a residential area, but when Finn arrived, the lobby of the building looked more like an art gallery with glass-paneled walls and abstract sculptures. He pinged a handsome tip to his Uber and then wondered if he should have asked her to park up and wait for the return drive. But he had no idea how long the conversation was going to last or what they'd end up talking about, since they only had Jasper in common. He wasn't even convinced that simply knowing this guy's name and address would grant access to the onyx-brushed elevator.

Determined, he flipped his anxiety the bird as he hustled up to the control pad and pressed the silver disc for apartment number 42. After a series of beeps, the video feed above him captured his portrait, and he took the chance to smarten up.

"Hello?" came a disembodied voice through the small speaker hole. "Uhh, I don't remember ordering anything."

"Well that's good, because I'm not selling," Finn responded and offered a placid smile. "I've come on the instruction of Evangeline Wight."

"Ah," the voice chirped, tone rising at least two octaves. "You're keen; I only just got off the phone with her. Come on up."

As soon as the line went dead, a loud buzz clicked the locking mechanism for the elevator gate. Finn walked through, shut it behind him, and took a deep breath as he sailed to the top floor. The interior décor stayed just as sophisticated and immaculate as the lobby, and once he found the right apartment, he rapped on the door and wiped his palms on his trousers. Things would work out fine. He was used to getting verbally creative during board meetings, and this was just another chance to hone those skills.

It wasn't long before the door swung open, and Finn didn't know what he'd been expecting to face, but it certainly wasn't a dashingly handsome olive-skinned man with an angular jaw, sky-blue eyes, and silky black hair.

"Hey," he said. "I'm Blayze, but you already knew that. You're Mr. Anderson, I presume?"

"Yes, but call me Finn," Finn said, sticking out his hand.

Once they shook, Blayze moved aside so Finn could step in and gawp at the gloriousness of his open-plan apartment. Everywhere his eyes touched, opulence followed. Colorful egg chairs hung from the ceiling, a gargantuan television was built into the far wall, and the marble flooring was so reflective Finn could pluck his eyebrows in it. There was even a damned snooker table tucked into the corner of the room next to an oversized minibar.

"Beer?" Blayze asked, already heading for the steel double-doored fridge in the kitchen.

"Sure." Finn rested his hands on the polished granite island, relishing its cool touch. "So, how long have you worked for Eva?"

"Hmm? Oh, Mrs. Wight? Only these last few weeks," Blayze said as he fetched two bottles of Bud and twisted off their caps. "It's an interesting position, and I find it quite refreshing to work for such a powerful woman."

Finn nodded his agreement, and when Blayze handed over the bottle, there was something to be gleaned from the expression on his face. It was almost like he wanted to say a lot more about Evangeline Wight, but something held him back.

The curious twinkling in Blayze's eyes seemed to get bigger and bigger, and before Finn could so much as tilt his head to examine it, the man was engulfed by orange flame. His entire body was literally on fire, and the heat was more intense than a medieval blast furnace. When Finn took an instinctive pace backward, he only just managed to catch his own scream.

"Not bad," Finn said, aiming for nonchalance as he raked his hand through his hair. In an attempt to keep his composure and not bolt for the door, he slugged half his beer and offered the flaming man an awkward grin.

How had he not already long predicted what the mage's power was? The guy's name was Blayze, for crying out loud. It couldn't have been more obvious.

"Well?" he said. By the power of context, it was clear Blayze was waiting for some grand showcase of Finn's power. What he got in return was a shrug and a surrendering of hands. "Aw, are you going to make me guess? That could be fun, I suppose. You're a Shifter? Or, no, maybe you talk to animals rather than becoming one? Wait, hold up, you look like one of those Self-Duplicators. I only just found out about those a month ago, can you believe that?"

"I…" Finn wondered how best to explain himself without getting a fireball to the face. "I'm not a mage."

The second the words fell on his ears, the hellfire swathing Blayze's body switched off like a faucet, and his eyes almost popped out of his skull. He opened his mouth to speak, but instead of adequately articulating his distress, he only managed a series of garbled groans.

"I'm sorry to spring this on you," Finn said. "I know it must be weird. But your secret is safe with me. I'm one of the good guys."

"There's no such thing," Blayze snorted, crossing his arms. "And I'm really not in the mood to have a containment squad rain down on my apartment just to wipe your memory. God damn, they're gonna kill me for revealing myself like that so carelessly. I've had a long day, and the last thing on my to-do list is to babysit a blip. You need to leave."

"A blip?" Finn repeated, trying hard to center himself and focus on his rapidly waning sense of direction. "Let's just chill for a sec. I know you don't know me and definitely don't appreciate me being all up in your business, but please don't toss me out or call the magic police or anything. Not without hearing my side of the story."

Blayze clicked his tongue impatiently. His body language was still on the defense, but the pause in his threatening tone was a good sign.

"It all started less than a week ago," Finn said, hoping that honesty would carry its own weight. "When I started receiving some messages on my mirror, I thought it was some kids playing a prank, but it was Jasper searching for help. Ever since meeting him, my very perception of existence has been thrown into an industrial mulcher, but now that things are starting to make more sense, I really need you to believe me. My interests in your kind are purely from a place of admiration, and I'm not hellbent on organizing the biggest coup in the history of Earth. Jasper's mom wouldn't have put me in contact with you if she had any shred of doubt about my intent. Right?"

Blayze produced a wry smile and finally relaxed his stance. Then he went to sit in one of the suspended chairs in the main room and indicated for Finn to join him as he took some time to process what was just said.

Clearly Finn had struck a chord by bringing up a hard fact. How would he even know about Eva if he was lying through his teeth? She didn't seem careless enough to let business cards slip out of her purse. Blayze was spot on when he said she was a powerful woman, and to that end, why would she send him here if she didn't want him to source this all-important magical tool? Even though Jasper was technically the one in the wrong for first making contact, she was doing her best to keep her son out of trouble, and Finn would jump at the chance to solidify a future with him.

Though he had lots more he wanted to say and it wasn't usually in his nature to hold back, Finn recognized the best thing he could do in that moment was wait for the man with the absently wandering eyes to draw his own conclusion.

"Let me see if I'm understanding this correctly," Blayze said, eventually leveling his gaze on Finn and straight up refusing to blink.

"Up until a few days ago, you had absolutely zero knowledge of the magical world and those of us who exist in it?"

"Nope." Finn shook his head.

"And now that you've beaten astronomical odds by stumbling across Jasper and experiencing the wonder of his cooking, you're actively choosing to roleplay as the pawn on this fucked-up chessboard where imbalance is more evident than the Leaning Tower of Pisa?"

"Um, I mean I wouldn't really put it like that but… yes?" Taking a moment to breathe, Finn didn't realize just how bunched up he was until he saw Blayze break free from his stoic interrogation position. "What's the big deal? Oh, I don't mean to sound standoffish, I'm only curious. Don't you have any human friends?"

"No," Blayze said quickly, almost as if he couldn't tolerate the notion for too long. "I mean, I might have friends who have human friends… but I don't make a habit of mixing with people who can't fully share my experience or allow me to be my authentic self. Doesn't make sense."

Finn nodded and felt his chest turning into lead. "Okay, although I think I get where you're coming from with that, you've gotta admit it's a pretty narrow worldview. There are billions of people who walk this planet. How many mages are there compared to humans? Actually, you know what, I don't think I need the stats."

"Maybe you do," Blayze suggested. "We've been around as long as the rest of you have. And we're still human, we're just blessed in certain ways, minus the religious connotations. I'm a little surprised you didn't know that already. Maybe it would do you some good to learn a bit about the world you're trying to force your way into. You realize that you won't ever be able to learn spells, right? No way, no how. If you've got that idea floating around up there, better get rid of it pronto."

"Look, man," Finn said, irritation getting the better of him. "I don't know who's put this jagged stick up your ass, but I'm not backing down just because you have preconceived notions about the intentions of every human being. I'm a straightforward man who lives a respectable life. Not once have I thought about whether I could learn a spell one day. Sure, I may not yet know all the ins and outs of your society, but what I do know is that I've stumbled across something extremely special in Jasper. I care for him a great deal, and I see something meaningful in our union. Obviously it didn't work out between you guys for whatever reason—I haven't exactly been begging him for the details—but by the sounds of it, this swearstone thingy is basically my one chance to pursue a future with him. Are you really going to be the reason that I don't get the chance to do that? All because of some age-old rules? Can you have something like that on your conscience?"

"It's called an Oathstone." Blayze sent his gaze to the ceiling again, then got up from his chair only to idly stare out of his window. "And it's my job to determine who is truly deserving of such a priceless gift. Why should I part with one of the most treasured artefacts of magekind to somebody who doesn't even offer it the proper respect? Also, for your information, I don't take kindly to emotional blackmail."

"Sorry," Finn said. "I honestly didn't mean for it to come across like that. Not gonna lie, I'm kind of spiraling here. The thought of losing him is one thing, because yeah, maybe we are two people from two different worlds that aren't ever meant to mix. If ya'll have managed to keep it a secret thus far, I'm sure you've got a good working model of how to conceal all things mage. But you know what I can't stand? I can't stand the thought of him disappearing entirely without a trace of him ever being there in the first place. And it's not just me that would get hurt in that process. Even if I remembered nothing, Jasper would still remember me, and I know it would pain him to see me carry on as if we'd never met, because the same is true in reverse. The things he's opened my eyes to have become too important to me as a person, and as cringeworthy as it sounds, he's renewed my passion for living. Things were tedious and insignificant before I met him. Now, he's basically becoming my sole symbol of hope, and I'll do anything it takes to keep him where he is until the day comes where he chooses otherwise."

Because Finn had been talking to the back of Blayze's head as he peered down at the city below them, his reaction was impossible to gauge. He might've even been point-blank ignoring the outright baring of his soul, but when he turned back around, that didn't seem like it was the case. Blayze must have listened to every single word and resonated with it on some level, as there was a single tear falling down his cheek, finding its way into his dark stubble.

As he crossed the room again, it looked like he was going to sit back down, but he took Finn by surprise again when he offered out his hand.

"You've evoked things in me that not many can manage. In spite of my steely exterior, I am a romantic at heart, and though I do miss that goofball, Jasper and I ended on amicable terms. He's a fine man and an even better mage. I've always lived to serve the flame, and right now, I'm very glad that I'm the latest in the line of Truth Watchers. If an Oathstone is what you guys seek to keep your flame alive, who am I to deny you?"

Delighted to hear it, Finn cracked a huge smile. He took hold of Blayze's hand and was hauled from the chair with remarkable strength. Then together they walked to a decidedly quieter portion of the apartment, where the only piece of furnishing was a mahogany cabinet engraved with hundreds of ornate carvings.

"We'll sort out the paperwork in a minute," Blayze said as he got on tiptoes to fetch a small golden key from the top of the dresser.

As he unlocked a drawer in the center and made a show of slowly pulling it out, his hands were trembling with excitement or fear or both. Finn was about to tell him to stop being so dramatic and get on with it, but the sentiment was lost as soon as he saw what all the fuss was about.

Nestled inside the drawer were five small crystalline stones whose color shifted on their own between ethereal blue and green hues. Each of them looked like they were living and breathing with their own personal sense of vitality, and in all of his years, Finn had never lain eyes on anything more alluring.

With his heart hammering in his chest, he reached out his hand and an almost magnetic tug warned him that things were about to change forever.

CHAPTER TWENTY

DOING SOMETHING as familiar as prepping food helped Jasper return to a relatively normal state of mind.

Courtesy of his gift, there was absolutely no need for him to shell the chickpeas for the hummus, but it felt good to have muscle memory kick in and do something laborious with his hands.

His little meltdown from before was just a blip—an involuntary test of his confidence in Finn. In hindsight it was probably a good thing it happened, especially while Finn wasn't around.

When all the ingredients were laid out in their pots, patiently waiting for the imaginary heat of his power, Jasper sat himself cross-legged on the couch and attempted a deep breathing technique he'd learned as a child. Meditation had never come easy for him, but it was the willingness to try that counted.

Before he could fully appreciate how much time had passed, his front door clicked shut, and he caught sight of a very befuddled-looking Finn. He had glassy eyes, and his movements were hesitant and awkward, almost as if he'd spent the afternoon with a ghost.

"You okay?" Jasper asked, undoing the knot of his legs, doing his best to circumvent the pins and needles. "That's a new expression on you."

"Weird night." Finn shrugged out of his coat and hung it up. Then he crossed the distance between them and planted a hard kiss on Jasper's lips. It was long, passionate, full of vigor and promise, and as Finn began to riffle his hands through Jasper's hair, Jasper backed off a little to catch his breath. "Are *you* okay?" Finn asked, eyeing him warily.

"Yeah, fine." Walking to the kitchen, hovering his hands over the food, Jasper was shamefully thankful to have an excuse to break eye contact for a moment. "So," he started, making a conscious effort to keep a lid on his darker feelings, "how'd it go? Did Gabe get a good investor to help out?"

"It was your mom I met, not Gabe."

Jasper's power ceased the moment he looked up. "What? Did I just hear you correctly?"

Finn nodded. "Yep. Your mom decided to spring a trap to corner me."

"Eh?" Jasper edged back around the counter in disbelief. "How does that…? Are you sure it was her? My mom?"

Finn snorted and one of his eyebrows tickled his hairline. "As if anybody could mistake your mom for someone else. She had Gabe text me to meet her in a swanky bar, and after she mind-controlled everyone to evacuate, she gave me the third degree and stiffed me with the bill."

"But why? What business does she have with you?"

Finn paused for a long moment, and just as Jasper was starting to wonder if he was deliberately holding something back, he flashed a radiant smile. "She just wanted to talk." He threw his hands up in the air and settled himself on the couch where Jasper had just been. "Sounds crazy, I know. But she simply wanted to know was what my intentions are with you, and I'm gonna go out on a limb and say that I impressed her. Things will work out. You'll see."

"Oh." Jasper stood with hands on his hips and stared into space. He couldn't remember a time when he'd felt equal measures of relief and surprise. He was very glad Finn hadn't spent half the night getting merry with his stupidly attractive coworker, but he had to wonder what his mom's real motives were. Surely not a cozy little chat?

"It was the weirdest thing," Finn said, "seeing her display her magic. Like, after she made everyone leave, they wanted to come back in after a while. As did new people… but there was an unseen force at the door keeping them at bay. Nobody could work out what to do except stand there with blank faces like they were attempting a sudoku written in kanji. It was so strange."

"I'll bet," Jasper said. His mother used her gift every day at work but only in small doses to make people help her in minute, subtle ways—never a full-on presentation of strong influence. In front of a knowing human, no less. "It just… it seems odd for her to go through so much trouble. I don't exactly trust her, in case you haven't noticed."

"Yeah, I got that. But maybe it's about time you did. She's got your best interests at heart, believe it or not. And how's about you dish that up, then?" Finn nodded his head toward the Middle Eastern spread. "It seems navigating people's bullshit has me famished, and I'm eager to try more of your food."

Kicking himself for being too busy overanalyzing to come up with anything flirty, Jasper didn't know what to make of Finn giving him advice on his very tenuous relationship with his own flesh and blood. But then Finn yanked at Jasper's collar to bring him down to his level and offered yet another bold, unforgiving display of affection.

The surprisingly needy kisses were more than welcome, and Jasper leaned into his warmth. He lacked both the energy and the desire to stay mad at Finn for long.

CHAPTER TWENTY-ONE

AFTER DEVOURING the best chili, nachos, and hummus dip he'd ever eaten, Finn sat on the couch to catch up with social media while Jasper arranged recently revived egg rolls into concentric circles.

When an email pinged through from his dad, Finn minimized Facebook and sighed dramatically. Judging by the text in the little preview box, it wasn't going to be a happy check-in. This mandatory interaction was bound to put Finn on edge, and he wondered if it was a smart idea to retreat to the bedroom for some privacy. But that was stupid. Even after eating half his body weight, Jasper was trying to make their business partnership work, and Finn should lean on him if needed.

The email wasn't seventeen paragraphs long, and Finn didn't know why he expected it to be anything less than concise. His father was never one to dance around the point, and there was no reason for him to be anything but direct. Still, Finn had been secretly hoping for a smidge of emotional understanding, and his heart sank when he skimmed the text and then reread it properly.

Finn, I am sure you must already know why I am writing you this email. It goes without saying that I am disappointed with your conduct of late, and it is also clear that your interests clash with the wants and needs of the company's future.

I am nothing if not a man of my word, and so, therefore, your position at Zest will be taken by Gabriel Fernandez, and your allowance will be cut off as promised. To avoid any confusion, this includes your place of residence. I have attached your severance

paperwork along with the regulations notice in accordance with what
you signed when I first loaned you the startup funds. You have a week
to move out and find your own feet. I truly hope that you do.

Sincerely,

A.A.

Finn howled with laughter, but there was zero humor in it. He
was upset—not because he'd lost the job but because of the monstrous
betrayal from someone he should've known better than to trust. He'd
worked twice as hard to keep his day job and entertain new project
ideas with Jasper.

Clearly, it was going to be a long while before he could have the
kind of relationship with his parents that, deep down, Finn realized he
actually wanted. As it was, Finn's dad could go fuck himself.

Being nothing besides corporate with them for years on end
had shoved any notion of family bonding out the window. At least he
finally knew where he stood. There was power in closure, and it was
strangely liberating to be done with all the bullshit.

"Hey, Jasper?" Finn closed the laptop, feeling a curious wave of
nervous relief wash over him. "Can I borrow you for a sec?"

"Uh-huh," Jasper muttered, violently munching an egg roll. "I
know I'm not supposed to eat the art… but I can't help it."

"You're adorable," Finn said as Jasper climbed on his lap. "So,
it seems I've just been fired."

He studied Jasper's reaction and found a mix of surprise and
anger and perhaps a twinge of happiness. "How can they do that to
you? Aren't you the part owner or something? Are you okay?"

"I'm fine." Finn was surprised to find that he was. He traced
a finger along Jasper's jaw and pulled him in for a quick kiss. "I'm
great, actually. Fuck that job. I checked out months ago."

Jasper nodded and ruffled Finn's hair. "Well, good. As long as
you're happy, that's what matters."

"In fact, to show I'm willing, let me just send a quick message."

He dove into his pocket and got out his cell phone. One-handed,
he typed a quick text to Gabriel.

Hey, I'm sure you heard the news by now. Believe it or not, I'm actually glad you'll be at the helm of the ship. You fit the lifestyle better than I do. Good luck, dude.

When he tucked the phone back, Jasper craned his head to kiss Finn's cheek. "I'm very proud of you."

"Thanks. But there is something that would make me happy...." Finn eyed Jasper's excited reaction again. "I know we've got this whole business thing on the horizon, but it's pretty clear that's only feasible when you get out of here. I've just lost my job, and I'm imminently about to be homeless... so, in the meantime... how would you feel if I made myself a little more comfortable?"

"Hah!" Jasper grinned ear to ear. "Are you asking if you can live with me?"

"That's exactly what I'm asking."

Jasper hesitated, and Finn had a long, painful moment of doubt. It had taken a lot of courage for him to let his guard down and lay his cards bare. A few weeks ago, he'd been set on never sharing his personal space with anyone ever again except for sex. But things had evolved since then, and he couldn't think of any place he'd rather be than by Jasper's side. And he, thankfully, had a promising smile on his face.

"If I'm being honest," Jasper started, "I was a little hesitant at first, even when I was starting to spy on you. You seemed like a carbon copy of everyone my mom used to set me up with. It takes a lot for me to get over people trying to use me—they've been doing it my whole life. Asking me to make a last-minute birthday cake or some fancy artisanal brownie thing then dropping me like a sack of shit afterward. But you're ticking all the boxes. Ordinarily I wouldn't rush into something like this... but for all I know, my time's limited. God knows what'll happen if I stay stuck here for the rest of the year."

"If that is the case," Finn said, "I'll stick it out with you for as long as it takes."

Tears began to well in Jasper's eyes, but Finn brushed them away.

"Are you sure?"

"Absolutely," Finn said with as much conviction as he could manage. Transparency and trust were key to any strong relationship. "I'm with you, Jasper, now and always."

"Thank you." Jasper took a deep breath, grinned, and kissed him. "I'd love you to move in with me."

His smile was infectious, and Finn couldn't keep his own grin at bay as he claimed Jasper's mouth. Jasper was too full of nervous excitement to keep his hands in just one place. First, he had them rooted in Finn's hair, letting his freshly conditioned waves loose to scent the air with citrus. Then Finn planted his hands on the small of Jasper's back to press his weight farther into his lap. Finally, Finn's hands ended up under Jasper's shirt and tweaked his nipples as Jasper moaned into Finn's mouth, urging him on.

They were so wrapped up in each other, so busy celebrating their union, that it took Finn all of five seconds to realize it wasn't Jasper making the chair vibrate. It was the whole apartment.

"Shit!" he bellowed, giving Jasper what was probably the fright of his life.

Then came a deafening crack, and Finn's heart nearly gave out when he realized what was happening.

"Earthquake," he announced. Jasper hopped up from his lap, looking horrified and standing too still. "Get to cover!"

It sounded more like the crackling of electricity than the booming shift of tectonic plates… but Finn had seen plenty of earthquakes back in Tulsa, and it was too similar, so when instinct finally kicked in, he pulled Jasper underneath the arch of the bedroom doorway.

He was prepared to huddle around Jasper and shelter him in case the archway fell down, but as soon as they got underneath, the vibrations stopped almost as quickly as they'd come.

"The fuck was that about?" Jasper asked, heading toward the window. "There's no damage in here or outside. In fact, nobody in the street seems bothered."

Finn had remained in place under the door, too fixated on what he was seeing. "That's because it wasn't an earthquake."

When Jasper followed his line of sight, he gasped. The front door was wide open, and its frame was shimmering with the remnants of an electric-blue energy. Both of them knew what it meant, and there was no denying what had to happen next.

As he walked up to the door, Jasper cursed under his breath. Then he passed right over the threshold.

Chapter Twenty-Two

AFTER MONTHS of being trapped in his apartment, Jasper was finally free. After countless hours listlessly dreaming about the warmth of sun on his skin, as it was intended and not just through a windowpane, he was able to do just that.

"Oh my God...." He sighed and looked from left to right. Never before had he been so happy to see scratched magnolia walls and poorly lit corridor.

As Finn, his brand-new roommate, came to join him, he sniggered when Jasper bent down and started stroking the carpet.

"This is awesome!" Finn shouted. "I guess you found inner peace after all?"

"I guess so." The giant grin on his face was probably proof enough, but Jasper tried to search within to see if he'd felt a more significant shift. "Maybe all of this was just the kick in the ass I needed. I feel more content with my path in life. Maybe it's because I finally feel safe enough to let someone in my headspace?"

"Don't be silly. It was beca—"

Jasper cut him off with a kiss. Whatever the real reason was, the joy shooting through his body was unparalleled to anything he'd ever experienced. It was as though Jasper Wight had been reborn as a whole new version of himself.

When Finn pried Jasper off him, he suggested he grabbed the apartment keys. "I know you've only just got out," he said, "but I'm assuming we would like to come back at some point?"

"Not anytime soon." Jasper felt an unwelcome wave of anxiety as he nipped back inside to grab the keys off the counter. He could've sworn they'd gotten dust on them because they hadn't been used in so long. "We're moving as soon we get the chance."

"Understandable." Finn beamed when Jasper jogged back outside safely. "So, what do you want to do first?"

When the door slammed closed, Jasper was at a loss for words. He stood in place with his head tilted as though he were watching a firework display.

"I don't know," he finally admitted.

Now that he'd beaten the snare, he had virtually no idea what to do with his freedom besides head straight for the staircase leading to the outside world. There were at least a thousand possibilities, a thousand new things to do with Finn that could bring them even closer.

"What's your favorite flavor of ice cream?"

As they reached the last flight of stairs, Jasper giggled at the random question. Then he realized Finn wasn't just asking to satisfy his ever-burning curiosity. Summer wasn't yet over, and he could actually go grab a cone—or six—if that's what his heart desired. He'd have to remember he could do things for himself now. He'd become dependent on other people, and he'd have to learn how to stand on his own two feet once again.

Paying Mikasa and Elijah's rent money back was a major priority.

"Berry ripple," he answered Finn, who rolled his eyes. "Hey! Don't go judging me! My granny used to make it homemade when I was little. Her secret recipe used three different types of berry, and every time I tried to replicate it with my gift, it was never the same."

"Cute. Well, I know a place," Finn said. "Wanna head over there and then see where fate takes us?"

Jasper nodded enthusiastically. He was delighted to see people milling around the lobby, so he made sure to greet everyone he saw. Finn laughed nervously as he dragged him to the door.

"Stop that," he ordered, pushing him out. "People will think you're crazy."

"Maybe I am," Jasper chirped, clutching Finn's hand as they found the sidewalk and danced to avoid streams of people. He felt like an ant against the glittering skyscrapers, and there were a thousand possibilities as the boundless city sprawled before them.

"Nothing's changed," he said while being led down Ninth Avenue. "It's still the busiest place on the planet, and I've never been so in love."

"Well, *some* things have changed." Finn squeezed his hand. "I wonder how different things will be between us now that you're out."

"Yeah," Jasper mused, wondering if their level of wariness matched.

It was like he was on day-release from being jailed for a decade. Everything felt too temporary, too surreal. The world might be cruel enough to snatch his liberation back at any given moment. But freedom was in his bones, and there were so many factors to consider now that their relationship wasn't limited to the same four walls. Now that they had an entire metropolis to play with, he sincerely hoped Finn would take the lead for the time being because he was positively stumped.

He'd learned a lot about both himself and Finn during the time he'd spent spying on him, but Jasper's forced involvement in Finn's life had no doubt caused him some strain, and his actions had been thrown off as a result. It was clear a modeling agency would snap him up in an instant for his muscles alone, but was he normally a chilled-out movie-marathon kind of guy? Or did he take hikes on the weekend? Did he prefer to date at restaurants or the theater?

There were countless things still to find out, but that's how dating worked on the outside—slow and steady. Half of him couldn't wait to begin that journey, and the other was scared that Finn had seen too many of his bad habits and they'd skipped right past the honeymoon phase.

"Here we are," Finn announced. He'd been oblivious to Jasper's inner debate, and he was holding open the door of a dessert café of modest size. The scent of freshly baked waffles and pancakes wafted through the light breeze and promised to lift his mood. "After you."

As Jasper let go of Finn's hand to cross the threshold, he realized there could be worse places to be trapped if it were to ever happen again. The parlor boasted at least fifty colorful flavors of ice cream, and there were chefs in the open-plan kitchen in the back cooking up pastries to be served underneath them.

Despite the pleasantly warm temperature outside, the line wasn't long, and Jasper could hardly wait to place his order. With so many combinations to choose from, it was like being a kid again, and it sent a rush of pleasure when Finn whipped out a gold Amex and said he could have anything on the menu.

Jasper would be a fool to turn down such an offer.

"IF I have another bite, I'll hurl."

Finn smiled and pushed the dregs of his mocha waffle around the plate as he typed one-handedly on his phone. "You certainly know how to put it away."

Jasper had eaten three strawberry-covered pancakes and a banana waffle and topped it off with two scoops of mixed berry ice cream. The flavor profiles lacked a befitting description, but his stomach was starting to regret the calories.

"Not as good as Granny's," he said, "but a close second."

When Jasper purposefully cleared his throat, Finn was still too busy tapping on his phone to make eye contact. He didn't want to pry and seem all clingy, but it was kind of annoying how he was more interested in his device than spending face-to-face time with Jasper now that he was finally free.

Who the hell was he texting?

"I think I need to walk this off," Jasper said, calling Finn back to the real world. "What say we head somewhere downtown? I've seen a serious lack of the city since coming here, and the views will be even better when the sun starts to set."

"Sure thing," Finn said as he tucked his phone back into his pocket and a waitress appeared as if summoned by magic. "All the good spots are on the way back to my place, anyway."

Jasper wasn't sure whether to be affronted or flattered by the assumption. He settled on the latter. They were an item now, and there was little point pretending he wasn't dying to see Finn's bachelor pad in person.

As they took a leisurely walk, the sun started to dip into late afternoon territory, and the ever-bustling streets of New York kept their charm. Jasper's sluggishness had been cured, and he was raring to go in more ways than one.

"We can always go for a walk later?" he suggested.

Finn's breath hitched, and Jasper was certain his intentions were transparent. Finn gripped his hand tightly as they crossed the street, and he held the door open with his foot when they got to his apartment building.

"Fancy," Jasper said as they stepped into a chrome-bedazzled elevator. He'd been so used to using steps all his life that he actually preferred to walk, but he wanted to maintain the sense of urgency. If he had any doubts, the elevator took care of that. Heat fizzed between them in the small space, and Finn had his lips on Jasper's the moment the door shut.

They smooched as the car whizzed up to the top floor, and he didn't give a crap if anyone buzzed to get on. Breaking free had turned him into a succubus with a thirst that was impossible to satisfy, but he kept trying.

When the elevator pinged, Finn took a key card from his pocket and punched it into a special slot. The car lurched as they flew to the penthouse, and the doors opened directly into Finn's living room.

Although Jasper had seen Finn's place many times through the grainy vision of his projections, and he looked forward to seeing it in person, he barely got a chance before Finn literally picked him up and carried him to his room.

"I want you *so* bad," Finn breathed into his mouth. "I need you."

"So take me," Jasper said, digging his fingers into Finn's curls. "I'm all yours. Do with me as you please."

Finn chuckled and then threw him onto the bed just like before. Jasper gazed up as Finn unbuttoned his shirt, not once breaking eye contact as he stripped down to his boxer briefs and climbed up onto the bed. Then he made short work of stripping Jasper, threw his clothes on the floor, and peppered kisses roughly across every inch of his skin.

CHAPTER TWENTY-THREE

FINN COULDN'T contain his longing as he explored Jasper's body again.

Last time was one for the books, but he was determined to go all the way this time. It felt appropriate to commemorate the inevitable loss of the penthouse where Jasper made first contact. Now that Jasper had broken free and was still at his side, Finn didn't mind losing the apartment… but it was a fitting place to make love for the first time.

As long as he had Jasper, he didn't need self-cleaning machines, a fancy towel rack, or any other gimmicks.

"I love it when you do that," Jasper moaned as Finn sucked one of his cute pink nipples and gently tweaked the other between his finger and thumb.

"Good," he whispered, grazing his teeth on it to test his limits. "I'll be sure to remember that when I'm buried deep inside you."

Jasper took a short, surprised breath, eyes glazed over with raw desire. Finn wondered if they should skip foreplay and get right to it. He hadn't had full-blown sex in at least eighteen months, and he was worried he wouldn't last long, especially since Jasper on his bed with an arm behind his head, exposing the tufts of armpit hair and raking a hand through his blond curls was art personified. As much as Finn wanted to make the moment last, his need for Jasper was too strong.

"You ready for me?" he whispered, leaning down to further the kiss and distract Jasper while reaching into a drawer for the condom and lube. "I'm so excited for this."

"Yeah, me too," Jasper whispered, finishing off the tongue-kiss with a peck, then looking all kinds of sexy as he absently grazed his teeth on his bottom lip. "Which way?"

"That depends how flexible you are, doesn't it?" Finn tore the rubber from the packet, ensuring he kept a level gaze as he fixed it on. Squirting some lube onto an index finger, he snaked it down to Jasper's perfect bare ass. "I've always wanted to fuck face-to-face and kiss. Think we could do that?"

"Sure," said Jasper, absently stroking himself. "I've never done that either. It'll be a great way to celebrate our commitment to each other."

Finn agreed wholeheartedly. When he was prepared enough, he was careful to lift up Jasper's legs and rest his ankles on his shoulders. Smiling, he teased the puckered muscle with his fingers. Since Jasper's cock bent upward slightly, this was going to make for an interesting position.

"All right," Jasper said, stroking Finn's pecs with his free hand. "I'm ready for you, Finn. Be gentle with me."

Nodding to show his understanding, Finn pursed his lips, then used his tip to find Jasper's entrance. The heartbreakingly beautiful mage was at his most vulnerable, so it was important to keep eye contact and reassure him that Finn was trying hard to ignore his instincts to ram it straight in.

"Up a little bit," Jasper said, guiding him to the right spot. "There! Right there."

Gently, Finn pushed forward, and they both groaned when his warm ass enveloped Finn's cock. He was halfway in, but he knew to take it slow. Jasper stopped jerking himself briefly when Finn bent down and was thrilled to find he could kiss Jasper with ease. After a long moment, he pulled back and studied Jasper's face as he sank himself in another inch.

Jasper's face was screwed up a little, probably biting the inside of his cheek because the pain hadn't yet crossed over to pleasure. Finn eased out a little and offered a heartfelt smile.

"We'll go as slow as you want, baby." He kissed the tip of Jasper's nose.

Suddenly, without warning, Jasper took control, forced Finn's head down with his hands, and kissed him with lust-crazed vigor as he pushed his ass all the way forward, driving Finn in deep.

"Christ," Finn said, huffing a breath. "You're so tight."

"I'm opening up for you," Jasper said, taking no prisoners as he drew their bodies closer still and let the sweat slick them together as Finn began to get into a rhythm. "In every way possible."

A moment later Jasper bellowed out from sheer ecstasy, and Finn knew he must be hitting his prostate. He tried to keep eye contact with him, but Jasper's were sealed shut, no doubt lost in a haze of pleasure.

His ass was the perfect combination of warm, slippery friction, and it took only a few minutes of pounding for Finn's thighs to start a familiar quaking. Taking Jasper was raw pleasure beyond anything he'd ever imagined, and even with a condom, he was lavishing every second of his unfiltered neediness.

Jasper moaned and pawed at Finn, and that was all he needed to reach the stars and explode, but he made sure to pull back and watch Jasper jerk himself to completion as he did.

"Oh yeah," Jasper whispered, shooting thick wads into his chest hair as his eyes bored a hole into Finn's soul.

"That was perfect," Finn said, twitching from sensitivity as he disposed of the condom. Then he gathered Jasper into his side and let him curl his head into his embrace.

"*This* is perfect," said Jasper. "I feel so safe and secure when I'm around you."

"I do too," Finn said. Kissing the top of Jasper's lemon-scented hair, Finn relaxed and let himself be utterly spent.

THEY SPENT the next half hour in bed, just holding each other.

Finn was glad they got to have sex in his penthouse for the first time. He was also eternally glad that despite the odds, they had become a couple during Jasper's unusual situation.

Now that he had broken free, Finn planned to make use of every second of his company—not just because he was afraid Jasper might get caught up again, but because he was an entirely new person, one with a hopeful aura and a face full of smiles. It was especially true now that they were still lying inert on the bed, utterly exhausted and unbothered.

"Wanna jump in the shower with me?" Finn asked. As endearing as the moment was, he craved cleanliness. It would be both sexy and a monumental victory for Jasper to come full circle and actually join Finn in the shower, where Jasper first haunted him.

"Yeah," Jasper said, still not quite back from dreamland. "But I'm still basking. Just gimme a sec."

Finn smiled. The effect he had on Jasper was incredible, and he never wanted to stop pleasing him. But he really needed that shower.

"Shall I carry you again?" he asked. "You weigh no more than a feather."

"All right, fine," Jasper said, yawning and stretching before Finn picked him up. They walked at an unhurried pace through the apartment, and when they got to the bathroom, Finn put Jasper down in the preprogrammed walk-in shower.

"Amazing," Jasper remarked when the water cascaded down his shoulders. "So, this is what it's like to live like you?"

Chuckling, Finn climbed in to join him. "Better to not get too used to it."

The shampoo dispenser was off to the side, and Finn deliberately brushed up against Jasper before he pumped some soap into his palms and lathered it into his skin.

There was something romantic about getting wet and clean with someone else. Doing it with Jasper was no exception. His senses woke up the more the scalding water rejuvenated his skin, and after Finn gave him a good scrub, Jasper repaid him in kind.

Towels had already been toasting on the warming rack, and while Finn had missed his home comforts while at Jasper's, it was incredible they could share the luxuries together, even if only for a short while.

He fetched bottles of iced tea and tried not to think about the financial future as they padded to the bedroom again.

"I've got some clothes you might like," he said. It was handy that they were basically the same size, with the exception that Finn's muscles warranted a slightly larger fit.

He rummaged through a drawer of the clothes his mom had given him six years ago but that he'd never had the stomach to wear or throw away. He found a short-sleeve shirt set in a yellow polka-dot gradient. The collection was daring and bold.

"Wow," said Jasper, gaping. "That's an awesome top."

"I knew you'd like it," Finn laughed and chucked the top to him. Then he found an outfit for himself. "I'm getting pretty hungry after spending all that energy. Do you still want to go sightseeing?"

"I do." He was acting shy all of a sudden as he got dressed in a pair of khaki cargo shorts. "I can go on my own if you think it's stupid."

"No, don't be silly. I totally get it." He rubbed his shoulders, easing some tension. "Maybe we can go a bit later, though. When it's really dark? I've got a surprise for you."

Jasper tilted his head and showed a hint of a smile. "You do? What is it?"

"It wouldn't be much of a surprise if I told you, would it?" Finn walked around to his side of the bed and wrapped his arms around Jasper's waist. "Do you trust me?"

"Of course," Jasper said without hesitation. "I'm just not big on surprises. My dad tried to plan a surprise birthday party for me once, but the surprise was that he'd forgotten to invite the other kids. You can imagine how funny that was."

Finn shook his head and hoped he'd get to meet Jasper's dad soon. "Well, I promise you'll like this one," he said, pulling him toward the door. "You should know by now that I don't make empty promises."

IT WAS just after 4:00 p.m., and the sun was casting a perfect salmon glow across the horizon as they tangoed through an exceptionally busy Central Park.

On his other hand, Finn's fingers were crossed. If this didn't go precisely according to plan, he was going to be seriously pissed off. He was already wrapped up in his head about memory wiping and the dire importance of carefully wording lifelong oaths… so this really needed to go smoothly.

"What's in the park for us?" Jasper asked despite already guessing five times. Now that he was free from the confines of his apartment, he was jitterier than if he'd downed fourteen Red Bulls. "Are we going for a picnic?"

"Just a shortcut." Finn took a mental note of the optimism in his voice and shelved that idea for a future date. "You have to wait and see."

He had wanted to blindfold him, but that seemed like overkill, and Finn knew Jasper wouldn't let him anyway. As they crossed the road, he simply prayed that the flamboyant signage for the pop-up shop wasn't an immediate giveaway. It was nestled between a lash studio and a wine store, anyway, so hopefully it was somewhat inconspicuous.

Finn breathed a sigh of relief when he saw Mikasa and Elijah waiting outside, holding up the concealing tarp as promised.

"Hey, guys!" Jasper called out when he finally noticed his friends. "What are you two doing here? Did you know I got free?"

"Well, duh. You're right here, aren't you? And isn't it obvious, dummy?" Mikasa said, unable to wait a second longer before yanking the sheet down to let the sight sink in. "This is the debut of *Scrumptious Sculptures*! It's your first exhibit!"

Jasper squinted and took a big sideways step. When the penny finally dropped and he realized the setup wasn't either an accident or some big joke, he turned back around to present the biggest grin Finn had ever seen on somebody's face.

CHAPTER TWENTY-FOUR

"I CAN'T believe you!" Jasper was so excited to have a real space to work that he jumped into Finn's arms. "How did you manage to get this arranged so quick?"

"Pulled a few strings," said Finn. "As per your instruction, Mikasa and Elijah have been helping me collect a bunch of castoffs from local restaurants, and I thought I might as well use the last of my dad's cash to fund an event that was actually worth a damn."

The closer he got, the better Jasper was able to appreciate the cleverness of the fruit-and-vegetable-themed façade. A peek inside showed rows of benches and three dozen empty cases for art yet to be created.

An art show without any art. How quaint.

"I know this is a lot of pressure...." Finn held open the door. "Crafting masterful pieces from scratch and everything. But I believe in you. Get to work, my little Michelangelo. This place will be full of hungry tourists in about an hour."

Bubbling with excitement, Jasper got his game face on when he saw the extent of the sleek kitchenette out back. There was everything from an induction cooktop to deep fryers and even a fridge. This temporary space must be primarily for cuisine-based enterprises, and for all intents and purposes, it was a fully serviceable kitchen for all the humans who would eventually come looking. He and his friends knew what he could do with his gift, so it was merely an inspirational art studio where he could make his magic work in peace.

Looking at the stacks of food piled up on the countertops, Jasper was pleased to see that his vegetarian note had been taken on board. There wasn't a bit of meat in sight, and he'd never been more motivated to get creative.

Picking up some mushy beets and horribly bruised apples, Jasper hovered his hands in the air, closed his eyes, and thought of the Empire State Building.

IN JUST the space of half an hour, Jasper had used well over half of the ingredients supplied. As he took a seat on the counter to survey his work, he nibbled on one of the Reese's Cups he'd taken from the assorted candy box at the side.

Finn popped his head in. "How's it going in here?"

Jasper lazily waved a hand at him. "I'm exhausted. Can you pass me a different candy bar, please?"

"Sure," said Finn, coming in and closing the door behind him. "This is… beyond incredible, Jasper. I'm so proud of you."

Jasper went gooey at Finn's approval. He'd been worried the sculptures lacked a point of view, but as he inhaled more chocolate and climbed off the counter, he fell into Finn's arms and reveled in his warm embrace.

"What's say we get these on sale?" Finn whispered. "Visitors seem to have turned up earlier than expected."

Jasper leaned back and studied the beaming smile on Finn's face. Then he gave him a kiss, and together they carried out the first piece and placed it in the case. It was a recreation of the Statue of Liberty carved from a combination of french fries, sweet potato fries, and thick steak fries.

"Wow, Jas," said Elijah. "That's some neat originality you've got there."

"Thanks," Jasper replied. "Can you help me with the rest?"

It only took a few minutes of combined work for the four of them to lay out Jasper's edible cityscape. Jasper himself knew the piece must be cohesive because it was impossible to say which particular recreation of New York's landmarks was his favorite. The eggplant Chrysler Building was particularly fun with its textured-almond rivets. But then, he also enjoyed the Rockefeller Center made out of cheese twists, the Botanical Garden rendered with ladyfingers and a custard lake, and the Grand Central Terminal erected from profiteroles and complete with spun-sugar windows.

Each individual piece had height as well as depth, and Jasper knew damn well that they tasted amazing.

As their first set of customers began to approach, he breathed a sigh of relief at the look of wonder on a small child's face.

"Wow," the mother commented, eyeing the eggroll extravaganza Jasper had made to look like the Brooklyn Bridge. "These are truly fabulous. Is everything edible?"

"Sure is," Mikasa chirped. "But each sculpture comes as one piece. You can't just have *one* eggroll. Where would be the fun in that?"

"Mommy!" The child tugged at her arm, head barely visible above the gingham altar. "I want eggrolls, Mommy!"

"All right, honey." She smiled dotingly and extracted a cash clip from her pocket. With her ivory blazer and "let me speak to your manager" haircut, Jasper got the impression the woman wasn't one to give in easily. Maybe his pieces were worth a damn after all. "How much for this one?"

Mikasa looked to Elijah, who looked to Finn, who shrugged and looked to Jasper.

"I'm not sure," Finn said. "We didn't get a chance to play around with prices. What do you think, Jas?"

"Fifty bucks sounds reasonable," Jasper said, fixing himself behind the counter.

"To start off the auction, he means," Finn cut in, pressing a hand on Jasper's shoulder. "Don't sell yourself short, gorgeous. This artwork is timeless, and anyone should be lucky to purchase it."

The woman seemed a little hesitant, but Jasper kept a nervous grin on his face as she and some others began to bid, quickly working up a competitive contest to seize the piece. Jasper had worked hard to conceive and produce everything that was laid out, and he hoped he wasn't ripping anybody off even as they started to bid into the hundreds. He wanted a fair reward for his efforts, but were his creations really worth setting people back that much?

Looking at Finn's encouraging smile, Jasper knew he had to believe in himself more. When it was the original woman who claimed victory, he was delighted to see the look on the child's face.

"We'll come back later and have it after dinner, honey," she murmured. "After we've taken some good photos of it, of course."

As they walked away, Finn gave Jasper a strong side-hug.

"See?" he said. "You're an instant success, just like I knew you would be, given half a chance."

"We knew it too," Elijah called as he arranged more offerings to show. "Maybe now that you're out, Mi-Mi and I can get our cut?" Jovially, he nudged Jasper with his elbow. "You owe us a fair bit of rent."

"Of course." Though he knew Elijah was only kidding around, paying his friends back had always been one of Jasper's highest priorities. "How much was the up-front rate for this space?"

When Finn arched an eyebrow that said *don't worry about it*, Jasper watched as a new set of patrons eyed up Jasper's beetroot tower. The shop was starting to get busy, but since everyone had been happy to come back at the end of the day to collect their pieces, the inventory was able to stay on show and inspire future customers.

"I know some of you will be bummed out," Finn addressed the overflow of people lining up in the sunshine. "But if you miss out on grabbing a piece today, we've rented the storefront for the whole weekend, and we'll be sure to have more pieces tomorrow."

That was exciting news to Jasper, and with every new bid, Finn took the opportunity to hand out business cards that directed people to a website Jasper vaguely recalled suggesting. He didn't know how Finn had such a good memory, but his coding ability was second to none. And apparently Mikasa had had a large hand in the design elements, so whatever was currently spread across people's screens was bound to be killer.

In that moment, Jasper was overwhelmed at the people surrounding him.

"This is insane," he said, close to tears. "I can't believe people are actually interested in my work. Stuff that *I* actually did! With my hands!"

"Yeah," Elijah agreed. "But that's not all. Look who's just fought their way through. It's your par–"

"Jasper Wight," came an unmistakable voice. He would recognize that tone of voice anywhere... but even as the mob parted and his parents came into view, Jasper had a hard time believing his feet were still on solid ground. They couldn't be here. How would they have known? He stole a glance at Finn, but he was busy showing off Jasper's work to more customers.

"How the...?"

"Pick your jaw up, son," Jasper's father said sharply. "We're in public."

His mom was dressed in her standard-issue indigo blazer and wide-brimmed hat, and his dad seemed to be experimenting with a new swept-back haircut paired with a commander's outfit.

Despite their last encounter, Jasper rushed around the counter to give his mom a hug. She smelled of gooseberries and jasmine, and she accepted the embrace, not about to be embarrassed in front of the lively crowd.

Jasper was delighted to find that she squeezed him back a little. "I'm sorry for the way I behaved," he blurted out. "I was going crazy stuck in that place."

"No matter," she said, a hint of humor in her voice. "Well, you did better than Sara, at any rate. She got trapped for almost an entire year."

"She did?"

"Yes, son." Jasper's dad was peering at the artwork. "Didn't you wonder why she didn't come home for so long?"

"I just thought she was at college...."

"Honestly, Jasper," said his mom. "You should pay more attention. If your head was any farther in the clouds, you might as well live up there."

When Jasper started to laugh, he realized it was the first time in too many years that he'd had any semblance of fun with his parents.

"These creations of yours...," started Jasper's dad. "Well, they're truly rather marvelous."

Jasper had no idea why his father had suddenly adopted a British accent, but it didn't matter. The words coming out of his mouth were too important, and Jasper gave Finn another side-hug by way of thanks.

"This is Finn, by the way," Jasper said to his dad. "He's been my rock these past few weeks. He really helped me when… others decided not to."

Though he was happy his parents had finally gone out of their way to show interest in something he was passionate about, Jasper couldn't hold back the dig.

"Oh, sweetheart, I'm sorry to have come across so cold," said Jasper's mom. "I feel remiss to have been so hard on you in the past. A big part of the mage's trial is to break out on their own without anybody mentioning that it's a test. A rite of passage, you might say. It's silly, I know. And I tried to help in my own way, but I must admit I could have gone about it a little better."

Admittance of guilt. From Jasper's mom. Never had he pictured the day.

"I take it you haven't yet asked your friends about their time during confinement?"

Turning his head, Jasper idly watched them handling customers. "But they haven't…."

"Yeah, we have," Mikasa called from afar. "Been there, done that. Never again, thank you."

Mouth agape, Jasper was amazed he could've been so blind. Not once had he thought to ask them. He'd just assumed his entrapment was a whole new thing. Suddenly, it all made sense why they'd been so generous and understanding with the rent.

Rolling his eyes to the shop's ceiling, he sincerely hoped his painfully evident naïveté wasn't a foreboding sign for his brand-new relationship.

"And you're all right with Finn?" Jasper asked, certain there had to be some caveats somewhere along the line. "As much as I'd like to believe otherwise, I doubt he tallies a perfect score on your two-hundred-bullet-point list."

Jasper knew his parents had never had an issue with his sexual identity. They had problems with the kind of guys he went for. Even now that Finn was dressed in a flamboyant T-shirt and cargo shorts, he had no doubt that they thought he was exactly the same as the rest—save the fact he wasn't able to shoot fireballs from his hands. There was no need for Jasper to tell his parents that, until a few days ago, Finn been the cofounder of a magazine corporation that had the potential for a healthy financial future and undoubtable social influence.

"Honey," Jasper's mom broke him free of his reverie. "The only reason I ever tried setting you up with people like your ex was because of his affinity with fire, like your father. Carrying on the family tradition was very important to me."

"*Was*?" Jasper repeated.

She nodded, smiling slightly. "Anyone who can make my son truly happy makes me happy also."

It was all very formal, and Jasper would have to apologize to Finn on their behalf for the embarrassment. But for now, he simply enjoyed the blissful irony. For the better part of two decades, his parents had been hellbent on setting him up with a powerful mage of high status. Now it seemed they were happy to let him choose his own path.

"What say we enjoy some Scrumptious Sculptures?" Finn asked, effectively breaking the silence. "Free of charge, of course."

Jasper's dad grunted in agreement as his mom eyed Finn. She probably knew that he was from a wealthy background just by the way he was conducting himself—that and she could sniff out money better than a bloodhound.

"Do let us know whether you'll be attending your sister's wedding, Jasper," she said, tearing into a panettone replica of Madison Square Garden. "Sara has grown even more exasperating while you've been away, if you can imagine that."

"I can, actually," said Jasper. "I thought I wasn't invited, anyway. My invitation seemed to have gotten lost in the mail."

"Don't be ridiculous," said Jasper's father. "I'll need some more men to make up the numbers. That mommy's boy she's marrying isn't half as talented as you."

If Jasper's eyebrows could shoot up any higher, they'd fly off his face, and the feathered rats outside would steal them for their nests.

"This is all well and good, but this?" Jasper's dad waved a finger between Jasper and Finn. "It's time you called it off. Your mother told you before that it could never last."

"Are you serious?" Jasper asked, mood plummeting from sky-high joy to rock-bottom anger in the blink of an eye. "Can't you just let things be for once? I'm finally happy, and I don't want it to end."

"You know the rules."

"Now, now," Jasper's mom interjected. "I told you before, Quentin. I've got it all figured out."

Scowling, Jasper set about enlightening another set of customers. For the next hour, he made a conscious effort to be amicable and try to put that past where it belonged, even if only to serve customers, eat the delicacies he'd created, and relish the compliments his parents were so long overdue giving him.

THE ART exhibition was a huge hit, and Jasper was overjoyed to find out the final figure when they totaled up all the cash.

"As well as a decent business seed, we could probably find a brand-new apartment with this," Jasper said, an ear-to-ear grin forever pasted on his face. "I still can't believe any of it. Especially that I've been so lucky to find someone like you."

"I didn't doubt you for a minute," said Finn. "What say we go somewhere? Just you and me?"

"I'd love to."

After the mild headache of such a roaring success, it meant a great deal to Jasper that Finn wanted to take him on a journey for just the two of them. They had been surrounded by the constant uproar of strangers for more than four solid hours, and while it was positively revolutionary for Jasper to finally feel confident in his work *and* get some cold hard cash for it, it was a good idea to spend some quality time with the man who had made it all happen.

After a few subway hops, Finn popped into a small independent store to buy himself and Jasper a can of peach soda. Instead of weaving past the constant stream of sightseers, they became two of them.

"This is probably the most romantic spot in the city I could think of," Finn said as they arrived at Brooklyn Bridge just before the sun was about to set.

Well… it's definitely working." Jasper gazed over the water as the last vestiges of sunlight started to sink beneath the matchstick skyscrapers. Sighing, he turned back toward the glittering city, ablaze with a saffron glow, the reflection flickering like flames on the East River.

"I can't believe I've never been to this bridge before," said Jasper. "In the few months I had in the city before I got trapped, I only went to and from work. Never got to visit any landmarks. It looks better in person than it does in my eggroll sculpture."

"Oh, really?" Finn said, face scrunched as he fiddled with something in his pocket. "I must've been to the Statue of Liberty no less than a hundred times. Visiting it with you will mean more to me than those times combined."

Shuffling down the bridge, a philosophical notion occurred to Jasper. Ambling across the city's most famous bridge and watching the goings-on of ordinary life right next to them drew myriad parallels about their relationship thus far.

Holding on to Finn's hand, occasionally stealing a quick peek at his gorgeously carved face, Jasper knew they had both overcome obstacles of their own. They had crossed a bridge between two very different worlds, and they had met halfway to join and create something powerful. It was clear that Finn had learned enough about Jasper that this would be close to his idea of a perfect date. It definitely beat doing tequila shots in a crummy bar watching the latest drag queen try to lip-sync her way to reality-television stardom.

"So, Jasper." They settled on another spot, this time at the midpoint of the bridge. "I've got something pretty serious I have to do right now."

"Don't tell me you're gonna jump?"

"Hah!" Finn chuckled. "Good one. I didn't realize you had such a dark sense of humor."

As Finn bent his torso in half to grab something from his pocket, his expression became sly. He had Jasper waiting in awe until he drew out a perfectly smooth gemstone that lit from a thousand corners.

Jasper knew exactly what the small glittering blue-green item was, and he couldn't find his voice for a whole minute.

"Finn? Where in the holy shitballs did you manage to get an Oathstone?"

Finn merely grinned. He held it in his hands, and it started to glow with an emerald fluorescence as he closed his eyes and forged ahead with an unbreakable oath Jasper had no idea the content of.

"As I am the one activating this stone, it is my purpose to uphold the oath that I, Finn James Anderson, am hereby making. For as long as I live, I swear to never reveal the existence of the magical community to those who aren't aware of its existence at the current point in time. It will be my duty to uphold this secret, and I shall never pass on pertinent or potentially compromising information should anyone ask."

After that, the glowing died away, and the bond was forged. When Finn breathed a very audible sigh of relief and tucked the spent stone back in his pocket, Jasper jumped into Finn's arms. "Oh, Finn! My parents are gonna be over the moon! Now you don't have to get your memory wiped!"

"I know," Finn crooned. "This locks in our happily ever after. And your mom was the one who arranged for me to get the stone, FYI."

"Shut *up*." Jasper's mouth fell open. "My mom? Went out of her way to hook you up with one of the rarest artefacts in the world? I think you have the wrong parent."

"It's true. She put me on track to acquire it when I met her the other day and asked about the stone. She's a very astute woman, your mother, and she must've seen or felt that I want more than anything to commit myself to you."

"Right. Well, that's…. I—I just can't believe she would facilitate something like that. The only thing she's ever given me were socks for Christmas, even though I wanted canvases and paint.

This is a huge freaking deal. So where did it actually come from if not her directly?"

"Blayze, one of your exes?"

"That tightass?" Jasper howled. "The only thing *he* ever gave me was chlamydia."

"Um, okay, anyways…." Finn's mouth curled up. "At first, I did think might be weird that an ex would do something so big in your world to help us out, but after I told him how much I cared about you, he said he was the latest Truth Watcher?"

"Truth Watcher? More like glorified rock keeper." Jasper cringed as if he had a bad taste in his mouth. "It's mostly clerical duties, he'll get bored soon enough. You need somebody higher up to sign off on the release of the stones, and I'm guessing that was my mom. Gah, I remember him always going on about getting a foot in the door with the MRF. He wouldn't shut up about how much good he would do in a position of authority. What a crock of shit. That settles it. They must be really scraping the barrel if he's employed by them and giving himself fancy titles."

Finn shrugged.

"Thank you, Finn. It means the world to me that you've made this promise."

Smiling to himself, Jasper started to tear up as Finn clutched his hand with a fierce grip and they began the leisurely walk back. Holding hands felt different now. It was the loving grip of a partner, and everything would probably be different now that they were finally unified.

As they neared their apartment buildings, the air between them charged with a fiery static. They were a pair. A couple. A force to be reckoned with. And the first thing on the agenda was heading back to Jasper's place for round two.

WHEN THEY got back to Jasper's apartment, Jasper wedged a cabinet against the inside of the door to act as a temporary fix for the busted lock. He'd get around to calling the super later. For now, he was finally able to let his lustful guard down as Finn shoved him to the bed, purpose written in the twinkle of his eyes.

"I wanna push some more boundaries," Finn said, licking his lips.

"Yeah?" Jasper knew too well what those soft pink lips were capable of, and he didn't have any regrets when he sealed his on Finn's.

"Care for a shower?" Finn asked. "Come on, dear." He got off the bed and let Jasper faceplant on the pillow and groan. "You can make it. We're still young yet. We've got many fun years ahead of us."

Although it felt as though his body were weighed down by lead, Jasper's inner drive wasn't about to let him get away with staying in bed and forgoing what could potentially be the best sex of his life. Finn, being the gentleman that he was, met Jasper halfway and supported most of his weight as they walked into the bathroom. Finn even picked him up and propped him in the shower as he turned the knobs to get the water working.

By now, there was no doubt that Finn wanted Jasper for himself—gift or any other magical stuff aside. His sacrifices hadn't gone unnoticed, and Jasper was appreciative of everything Finn had done for him.

Now that they were both stark naked, bodies pressed up against each other, with hot water running over their bodies, Jasper's need was paramount, and it was his turn to be selfish.

"How long's it been since you bottomed?" Spinning Finn around, Jasper kissed the nape of his neck and gently stroked his asscheeks with one hand as he lathered soap across those impressively taut pecs.

Finn chuckled and managed a small shrug. "I honestly can't remember. Like, eight years or something? Too damn long, but I haven't been with anyone who I wanted to in all that time."

"Whoa," he said, giving Finn's shoulders a gentle squeeze. That was a long time, indeed. Jasper had owned cars for less time. "So, do you want to?"

"Yes," Finn replied, turning around. The conviction in his eyes was undeniable. It wasn't just lip service to please Jasper—Finn actually wanted to share the experience. "I want to be with you in every sense of the word."

"Me too," Jasper said, offering a deeper kiss, pressing their wet bodies together. "I'll be forever grateful I met you."

"As will I." Finn brushed Jasper's cheek with his finger. "I'm so glad your ghost came to scare the crap out of me that day."

Jasper rolled his eyes, smirking. Turning Finn around, Jasper sunk to the bottom of the bath and pushed Finn forward. As the hot water trickled down his perfect body, Jasper spread Finn's cheeks and began to swipe with his tongue.

"Damn," Finn moaned, voice far away, reverberating in the small space. "I forgot how… *insanely* amazing that feels."

Jasper laughed, being as gentle as he dared so as not to spook him. He didn't want Finn to move an inch.

"Be gentle with me," Finn pleaded when Jasper reached into the cabinet for a rubber.

"Always," Jasper said, stroking Finn's back.

It was still a mindfuck for Jasper to have his man open to him when he'd been so dominant thus far. And yet it was perfect for them to trust each other enough to swap roles.

He pumped some lubricant in the palm of his hand and watched as Finn spread his hands out against the wall, certain he wasn't imagining the longing as Finn slowly edged his way back. The guy was practically begging for it.

It was easy to see where Finn's entry point was in the broad artificial light, but Jasper was merely teasing him as he rubbed the area, getting him mentally prepared. "Are you ready?"

"I am," Finn assured, wiggling his ass.

Before he went in, Jasper wanted to test something. Ever since Finn had gifted Jasper the beautiful bracelet, his magic had taken on a different level entirely. Even before he made the attempt, he knew exactly what was going to happen.

Power thrummed out of his bracelet-clad wrist, and Jasper closed his eyes as he breached Finn's hole and channeled the brunt of his inner energy to transport them to the misty haven of the astral plane.

"Man!" Finn gasped. Jasper wasn't sure whether it was from shock or pain or both, so he pulled out and gave him some room to breathe. "We're in the plane?" he asked, too damn smart for his own good.

"One of them, yeah," Jasper said. He'd succeeded at transportation for the first ever time. With a human too. He was damn proud of himself. "It's pretty weird, isn't it?"

"You could say that," Finn said, looking around the ghostly version of the shower cubicle. "It feels incredible. What you're doing back there, I mean. It's like the best kind of fire."

With that, Jasper inched in again. Finn was impatient and took matters into his own hands by sinking himself all the way down on Jasper. Since he was permitting its very existence, the heat of the shower coincided with the delightful warmth of Finn's ass as it swallowed Jasper's length.

"Damn, Finn," Jasper giggled. "You old pro."

Finn laughed too, and it sounded genuine, not forced. He was obviously keen to be back in the saddle.

Grabbing Finn's shoulders, Jasper worked himself deeper. Finn's wet hair sent spray flying when he tossed his head back and began to moan a carnal, ethereal groan.

In all his life, Jasper had never topped anyone, so it was yet another new experience for him. If it always felt like his length was being gripped by a velvet vise, he doubted there was a chance he'd ever not want to flip the script again. His feelings for Finn went deeper than he'd ever thought possible.

In such a short space of time, Jasper had learned to be comfortable around a powerful, imposing man. During his many years of study, he had never once read about enhancing his gifts with a physical constant. Finn, being his usually cute self, must have spent ages ransacking all sorts of corners on the internet to get that information. Was Jasper among the few privy to such knowledge? It put him at the top of his game for the first time in his life, and he was finally in a headspace safe enough to be unafraid to be his authentic self. There was no doubt that Finn felt the same.

They were made for each other, and Jasper had been destined to project into his apartment.

"I love you," Jasper said, cast away in an ocean of ecstasy as he slapped his ghostly flesh into him.

"You do?" Finn asked, head reared back.

Jasper slowed down the pounding when he realized what he'd just said. But it was the truth. He'd spent the longest time believing he would never find someone who could support him in the ways Finn could. It was almost too good to be true to be buried balls deep inside that man.

"I know I can be weird and erratic sometimes," Jasper spluttered, "but I promise to always be there for you when you need me."

Jasper feared he'd made a grievous mistake in judgment, but when he pulled out, Finn turned his head and Jasper found him beaming with joy.

"Chill, dude," Finn breathed. "I love you too. You've changed my world for the better, and there's no going back after knowing what I know. Even if I didn't have the Oathstone, I'd still risk my memory getting wiped if it meant I got to spend one more day with you."

They latched on to each other's mouths in a harmonious fusion of body and mind. Fucking Finn had been thrilling and sensual and euphoric, but holding his face and caressing tongues elicited soft moans of appreciation, and nothing was sweeter than earning his trust.

When Jasper took the condom off and tossed it aside, neither of them had to touch themselves as they simultaneously exploded of their own accord, sending ribbons upon ribbons of raw pleasure into the ether, forever unifying their bond and sealing their astral connection.

EPILOGUE

WITH FINN'S business acumen, his promise was quick to come true. Scrumptious Sculptures was an instant hit and swiftly became the talk of New York. Within a week of setting up the exhibit, fruit of his labor could be found front and center in exclusive boutiques all over town.

People came from across the country to see Jasper's edible recreations of famous cities. Mikasa managed the Instagram page that buddied up with the website. She claimed it had a million followers in just three weeks, and Jasper began to receive commissions by the hour.

Exhilarating as it all was, mainstream success had its own drawbacks. Utterly wrapped up in each other, Finn and Jasper had moved into a modest two-bedroom apartment, and while it was fun to watch the ex-millionaire deal with ordinary stuff like using a washer-dryer and making his own coffee, talk of finances seemed to always make its way home. Bickering about petty subjects was foreign territory for both men, for neither had been in long-term relationships—much less lived with anyone else outside of a college dorm. But it was healthy to air problems as soon as they arose, and arguments were bittersweet because they were both glad to see a steady future after Jasper's escape.

Instead of outright disregarding him, Finn's parents grew to respect his new path. His dad probably recognized his son's need to distance himself and that he was finally able to stand on his own two feet. They even went on to schedule lunch dates once a month, which didn't immediately make a huge dent in the years of repression...

but it was a start. Whether it was down to guilt or Finn's booming prosperity, he couldn't be sure—the chats tended to focus on internal family matters rather than profit now that both Gabriel and Madison had been let go from *Zest* due to gross misconduct.

Quietly pleased with karmic justice, Finn didn't ask for the specifics.

Following their indisputably impressive achievements, Jasper was placed under investigation for a short time. The Force even interrogated Finn late one night, grilling him about how it was possible for his partner to craft such exceptional pieces without so much as an art degree. They were keen to confirm that Jasper had let his secret loose, but after making his oath, Finn simply showed them the Oathstone he had been wearing around his neck every day since a reputable jeweler had fashioned it into an amulet.

Now that Jasper's parents were proud of him and Finn's were finally showing interest in personal matters, the men were content to start living without worry. The roller coaster of everyday life was bumpy at times, but one thing was certain—neither could wait to find out everything there was to know about each other and watch their relationship blossom.

It was easier to make friends now that they were two, not one, and while it was thrilling for Jasper to introduce Finn to other mages and experience all the extraordinary things they could do, Finn knew in his bones that not all of them were content to stay in hiding. He couldn't help but wonder what it would be like if things were different, if there were a safe space where mages could reach out to approach potential soulmates, just like he had.

If only there were an app for that…

Keep reading for an excerpt from
Book Two of the CharmD Saga
Wishborne
by Sebastian Black!

BECAUSE THE bar was practically empty, Dane returned his glass and made sure to grab another drink before heading out to the garden. As he lit up, he was eager to track the progress of all the gorgeous fish in the koi pond, but he stopped in his tracks when he spotted a different kind of beautiful specimen—Blayze.

He had one leg crossed over the other, phone and drink on the table, and was vaping a small pen device. The frown on his face also suggested he was unhappy about something. Either that or he had a serious case of resting bitch face. Even though Dane very much wanted to sit next to him, stick out his hand, and introduce himself like the good old times, the fear of rejection made him linger.

Argh. He had to be tough with himself. If Ollie hadn't taken a chance on Dane when he was sitting in that exact spot, he'd never have met his current friends. He had to put on his big-boy pants and bite the bullet. Seize the day. Suck it and see.

"Your clouds smell funky," he said, taking a perch. "Is that real weed, or just flavored juice?"

"It's the real deal, but it's strictly medicinal," Blayze said, back tensing up a little. His leg started to bounce on the spot, and he offered a small smile and kept eye contact. "Helps keep away the crazy."

Smiling purposefully but not so much that it came across creepy, Dane angled away the smoke of his Marlboro in case it offended. "How'd you get it over the border?"

He shrugged nonchalantly. "Think they've got other things on their mind at the moment. Won't be long before you guys have it over here, I guess?"

"Maybe. I mean, I vote Green, but that's mostly 'cause they stand for environmentalism and anti-racism. Grass has lots of validity for being legalized, though I can't say I've ever actually partaken."

Blayze turned up a corner of his mouth and held out the stick. "Have a try. It's key lime pie flavor."

"I'm good, thanks." Tapping his glass, Dane was immensely proud of himself when he sent along a cheeky wink. "Probably best to stick to one vice for the time being, you know?"

A part of him wished he could match the blasé attitude, and when he pictured himself getting intoxicated and confident enough to do a whole host of things to those extraordinarily full lips, he had to consciously look at Blayze's eyes instead.

"So," he started, wishing he didn't have to pause so often to gather his nerves. "Is it just Blayze? Or do you have a surname?"

"Just Blayze," he said firmly. "And you're Dane Peterson, right? Don't worry, I'm not a creep or anything. It's on CharmD."

"Oh, of course." Dane grinned sheepishly. "I should know better than to put my full name on these things, but I like being upfront. Things tend to run smoother. Anyways, how are you enjoying London so far, Blayze?"

Blayze gave a little chuckle, then sighed softly. He uncrossed his leg, put the vape in his pocket, and reached for his beer. "It's a gorgeous place, but I expected it to be a little… I don't know… jazzier?"

Dane nodded and took another puff of his cigarette. "Yeah, I get you. Most gay bars have gotten distinctly less queer over the years. Think maybe the pink pound isn't worth all that much anymore."

"Possibly. Unless it's pride season, of course."

"True, true." His phone pinged—probably Terri wondering what was taking so long. "In terms of colorful people, I seem to find the mage gatherings bring a lot of eclectic tastes to the table."

"Oh?" He turned to face Dane head on, clearly intrigued. There was a spark of shock in his sky-blue eyes, and Dane abruptly got the idea that this guy wasn't quite as confident as he wanted everyone to believe. "Only been to a handful in the States. For whatever reasons, there's always a weird political undercurrent that I've never been keen on."

"Hmm," Dane offered. "Doesn't really happen here. It's more of a psychedelic rave, in truth. I'm still in two minds about going tonight. My mates think it's all well and good, but… well… I'm sure you know more than anyone why it's probably a silly idea."

"Maybe that's why we should go?" Blayze said. "As an act of defiance. We as a community have to stick together, don't you think? While I have no idea what's on the horizon, I get the feeling we might need each other real soon."

He wasn't at all wrong, and Dane found the obvious *we* mention very interesting. Either this Blayze guy was actually super into him and already inviting himself to things, or he was already sick of the bar and wanted to find some party action. In either case, over the course of their chat, his smile had gotten bigger, more genuine, and he had relaxed his body considerably—all good signs.

As desperate as Dane was to know what he could do, asking about someone's power was kind of taboo until you knew them well enough. It was like shaking a bus driver's hand after they've dropped you off. Doable, but weird. Mages preferred to show their abilities rather than speak plainly about them, and since they were out in the open of a nonsafe space, he'd simply have to wait.

He bet it was something powerful—useful, fun, creative.

Dane took another pull of his smoke; he was almost down to the label. When it was gone, he'd have no real reason to stay out here, so he needed to be daring.

"Wanna come, then?" he asked. "To the gathering, I mean. I think you're right about sticking together, and my friends have been badgering me for weeks—they aren't gonna let me dip out. If you come with, it's bound to be a lot more fun."

"Uhh, okay." Blayze winked. "Sure. Why the hell not? What's the worst that could happen?"

In celebration of his extroverted victory, Dane downed the rest of his drink simply so he could offer to buy Blayze's next one. He had a grin plastered on his face as they made their way back in, and despite all of the unspoken controversy and uncertainty, he felt good about his chances, and he was hopeful that this was going to be a fun night. Best yet, if Blayze had never been to a British mage party, he wouldn't know his ass from his elbow.

What had he gotten this poor guy into?

As soon as he discovered the romance genre, SEBASTIAN BLACK was hooked. From Rowling to Tolkien, from E. L. James to Stephanie Meyer, meaningful bonds can be found in the most unlikely genres. Though Sci-Fi and Fantasy are Black's top picks, they can't be without romance. Daring heroes and compelling heroines are what make fiction come alive, and when he began his writing career, "balls to the walls" quickly became his mantra. All writing should be tackled fearlessly. You can create a gourmet meal from the measliest of ingredients and seasonings, but you can't do much with a blank page!